Louisa the Ballerina:

Louisa's Secret

A Rival for Louisa

Louisa in the Wings

www.**kidsatrandomhouse**.co.uk

Louisa the Ballerina:

Louisa's Secret
A Rival for Louisa
Louisa in the Wings

by Adèle Geras

Illustrated by Karen Popham

RED FOX

LOUISA THE BALLERINA
A RED FOX BOOK 0 09 946397 0

First published as separate editions in Great Britain in 1997 by Red Fox,
an imprint of Random House Children's Books
New Red Fox editions published 2000

This 3-in-1 Red Fox edition published for Scholastic 2003

1 3 5 7 9 10 8 6 4 2

Papers used by Random House Children's Books are natural, recyclable products
made from wood grown in sustainable forests. The manufacturing processes
conform to the environmental regulations of the country of origin.

Red Fox Books are published by Random House Children's Books,
61–63 Uxbridge Road, London W5 5SA,
a division of The Random House Group Ltd,
in Australia by Random House Australia (Pty) Ltd,
20 Alfred Street, Milsons Point, Sydney, NSW 2061, Australia,
in New Zealand by Random House New Zealand Ltd,
18 Poland Road, Glenfield, Auckland 10, New Zealand,
and in South Africa by Random House (Pty) Ltd,
Endulini, 5A Jubilee Road, Parktown 2193, South Africa

THE RANDOM HOUSE GROUP Limited Reg. No. 954009
www.kidsatrandomhouse.co.uk

A CIP catalogue record for this book is available from the British Library.

Printed and bound in Great Britain by
Cox & Wyman Ltd, Reading, Berkshire

Louisa's Secret

For Miriam Hodgson

Chapter One

1 have to take good care of my legs and feet because when I grow up, I want to be a ballerina. I've been going to classes for three months now, and I've already danced in a show, so I'm a sort of ballerina already. Mrs Posnansky, our neighbour, says I am. She always calls me 'Little Swan', because that's what I was in the piece my class performed. Mrs Posnansky is from Russia, and her mother was in the corps de ballet, ages and ages ago, so she ought to know who is a real ballerina and who isn't. When I was being a Little Swan, she gave me the feathered headdress her mother used to wear, and she said I could keep it for ever and ever. I put it in a special box at the bottom of my cupboard, and it's my Very Favourite Thing.

If I didn't have to take care of my feet, I would have kicked my sister Annie under the table at supper. She called me Weezer. She *keeps* calling me Weezer, and I wish she wouldn't. I've explained to her over and over again that it's not the kind of name a ballet dancer would have. Louisa is my real name, and I don't see why she can't use it.

"Louisa Blair," I told her. "That's my name. It's a very good name for a dancer."

"I'm sorry," she said. "Only I've got used to Weezer. I've called you that for seven years, so it's hard to change all at once."

"You've got to try," I said. "You've got to get used to Louisa."

"OK," said Annie. "Louisa it is."

There was something very important I wanted to talk to her about. I said, "Were you here when they moved in next door?"

"No," said Annie. "I was at school, like you."

The house next to ours had been for sale for a long time, but it was sold a couple of months ago, and since then, I'd spent hours imagining the kind of family that would come and live there. I wanted them to have a child: someone I could play with, maybe even someone who could come to ballet class with me. I wanted them to have a pet, so that our cat, Brad, would have a friend as well. I used to discuss all this with Annie, usually while we were lying in bed, waiting to fall asleep. She said once, "Perhaps a handsome widower will move in, and Mum can marry him."

"Then he'd be a sort of dad," I said, "and we've got a dad, even if he and Mum are divorced. What do we want another one for?"

"Ours lives miles away," Annie said. "And I think Mum gets lonely sometimes."

"No, she doesn't," I said. "She's got us, hasn't she?" I didn't want to talk about Mum, so I said, "What will we do when the new people move in? Will we just go round there and knock at the door, and invite them to our house? I don't want to go on my own. We'll go together. OK?"

"OK."

"Promise?"

Annie sighed. She sighs quite a lot when I'm talking to her. "I promise. Go to sleep, Weezer."

"LOUISA!"

"Sorry . . . Louisa."

That was a few nights ago. Now I said, "Do you think we can go and say hello?"

Mum was in the kitchen, and she didn't wait for Annie to answer. "Certainly not," she said. "They'll be busy unpacking and getting everything straight. Tomorrow will be time enough for visits."

"But what if they've got lots of little kids all getting under their feet? They'd be glad to have them coming here for a bit, wouldn't they?"

"They haven't got lots of little kids," Mum said. "They've only got one, as far as I could see."

"A girl?" I held my breath and crossed my fingers behind my back for good luck.

"'Fraid not," said Mum. "A boy. With very dark hair."

I sniffed. I didn't care what colour his hair was, he was still a boy. "He won't want to play with me," I said. I'd have to stop daydreaming about a new friend.

"Why ever not?" Mum asked. "Boys like playing too, don't they?"

"Most of the time they like playing with other boys though, don't they? And I can't play football and climb trees, can I?"

"Why not?" Annie asked. "You used to like doing things like that. You're a fast runner, too."

"That was before I started ballet. I can't do those things now."

"Why not?"

Did she *really* have to have everything

explained to her? "Because," I said, "I mustn't injure myself. You can't dance if you're injured. And anyway, I haven't got time. I have to practise every day."

No one who isn't a dancer understands properly. They say they do, but they don't. You have to do exercises EVERY SINGLE DAY. The class is once a week, and lots of people who go to it do the barre exercises in class, but I do mine every single day, and sometimes I do them twice. In every book I've read about real ballet dancers, it says that you have do this if you are a 'truly dedicated dancer' and that's what I am. Even Tricia and Maisie, who are my very best friends, only really like going to class so that they can chat to everyone and dress up in satin shoes and pink leotards and things. When they come to my house, I make them join in dances I've made up, but I know they don't spend every spare minute thinking about being famous. They've both told me what they want to be when they grow up. Tricia wants to be a vet, and Maisie wants to be a nurse. I'm the only one who is determined to be a Prima Ballerina.

"Look!" Annie said suddenly, interrupting my thoughts. "Weezer, he's in the garden.

Come over here."

I was in such a rush to see our new neighbour that I forgot to tell Annie off for calling me Weezer. I stood next to her and stared out of the window.

The boy was small, about my size, and skinny, and he did have very dark hair.

"I wish he'd turn round," Annie said, "then we could see his face."

"I'm going out to talk to him," I said. "Are you coming?"

"No, you go by yourself. Go on. He might be a bit nervous if there's two of us."

"I don't see why he should."

"He shouldn't but he might. Go on, you go. Find out what his name is."

The boy didn't look like someone to be scared of, so I went. The hedge between our garden and his garden was quite low, so I could just see over the top.

"Hello," I called out. "My name's Louisa Blair. What's your name?" I wasn't scowling.

Annie says I often scowl, so I made sure to smile my very best and friendliest smile.

The boy turned round. He had a nice face, for a boy, with blue eyes and pink cheeks. He looked a bit nervous, but he was grinning (sort of) and he said, "Tony. I mean that's my name."

"Tony what?"

"Tony Delaney."

"How old are you?"

"I'm eight. Are you eight?"

"Nearly," I said. "I'm very nearly eight. Have you got any brothers or sisters?"

"No. Have you?"

"Annie's my sister. She's ten. Have you got any pets?"

"No. Have you?"

"We've got a cat called Brad. It's short for Bradman. You'll see him soon. He likes your garden. What school do you go to?"

"I'm staying at St Cuthbert's for this term. That's the school I went to when we were in our old house. Then next term, I'm starting at Fairvale Junior."

"That's my school!" I said. "It's nice there. You'll like it."

"I won't know anyone," Tony said. He looked sad.

"You'll know me," I told him, but it didn't seem to cheer him up much. I added, "You can come and play in our house if you want."

"Really?" He looked happier at once. "I'll go and tell my mum."

He ran indoors and so did I. "He's coming," I said to Annie. "He's coming to play. I invited him. Is that OK, Mum?"

"Fine dear," Mum said. "Give him a drink and a biscuit when he gets here."

Chapter Two

You *can* be friends with a boy. I didn't think you could, but you can. It all depends on the boy. Tony is a very good person to have as a friend, and because he lives so close to us, it means we can spend a lot of time together, either in his house or in mine.

"You really like him," Annie said to me one night, after he'd been living next door for a couple of weeks.

"So?" I said. "So what? What's wrong with that?"

"Weezer's got a boyfriend . . . Weezer's got a boyfriend . . ." she started to chant. I couldn't believe how stupid she was! *And* she'd called me Weezer! I threw my hairbrush at her, and it hit her on the shoulder.

"Oww!" she cried. "That hurt."

"Then stop being silly. Of course Tony isn't my boyfriend. He's a friend of mine, that's all.

And DON'T call me Weezer."

"All right," said Annie, jumping into her bed and pulling the duvet up to her shoulders. "Honestly! Can't you even take a joke?"

While I was falling asleep, I thought about Tony and why I liked him so much. There were three main reasons:

1. He always played any games I said we should play.

2. He didn't think boys were better than girls.

3. He never got cross, whatever you said to him.

"He's coming to play tomorrow," I said to Annie. "We're going to make a den at the bottom of the garden. It'll be our secret place."

"How can it be secret," Annie asked, "if you've already told me about it?"

"You must promise not to tell anyone. Do you promise?"

"OK," said Annie. "Now go to sleep."

We didn't make the secret den the next day. It was pouring with rain.

"We'll do it another day,"
Tony said.

"I wanted to do it today," I
said. I really hate it when I can't do
what I want to do when I want to do it, but
Tony never seems to mind a bit. I felt quite
annoyed with him. I said, "What are we going
to do instead, then?"

"We can play board games," Tony said.

"I hate board games."

"Then I'll show you some
card tricks."

"Don't want to learn card
tricks."

"Come
over to
my house
and we'll
play some com-
puter games."

Tony was better
at computer games
than I was, but I
felt silly saying no
over and over again,
so I agreed.

Tony's house looked like our

house, but it was much tidier.
Mrs Delaney is much fussier
than my mum, but I like her.
For instance, in Tony's house, we
can't take drinks or biscuits or anything up to his room. We have to sit in the
kitchen and eat properly at the table.

Tony loves his computer games, but I can
never see the point of them. All these little
figures just race about on the screen, and you
have to zap them. I asked Tony,
"Why do I have to zap them?"

"Because they're the
baddies. And the more baddies you zap the
more points
you get."

I zapped
for a while,
but it soon got boring.
"I know," I told Tony,
"come back to my house
and we'll watch videos."

"What videos have
you got?" he asked.

"All sorts," I said. "Come on."

"OK." Tony switched the

computer off, and followed me to our house and into the lounge. There he was, agreeing with me again. Why didn't he care whether he got his own way or not? I decided to ask him. I said, "Tony, why don't you mind what games we play or what we do?"

He thought about this for a few seconds, then he said, "Well . . . I suppose it's because I like doing most things . . ." His voice faded away.

"Don't you ever get cross and lose your temper?"

"Sometimes I do."

"When was the last time?"

"Years and years ago."

"Years ago? That's amazing!"

"Why is it amazing? When did *you* last lose your temper?"

I laughed. "Yesterday. Or maybe even this morning. I can't remember. I get cross all the time."

"You've never been cross with me," Tony said.

"That's because you let me do everything I want to do. And what I want to do now is watch this video. It's very special. You sit there and don't say a word."

Tony sat on the sofa. He was looking excited, and I felt a bit bad about the trick I was going to play on him. I knew he thought he was going to see a film. I knew he was going to be disappointed, but I thought the best thing was just to start the video going and hope for the best.

"What's this?" he asked after he'd been watching for a few seconds.

"It's my new ballet video."

"Your *what*?"

"Ballet video. It's special. This is a film of Rudolf Nureyev and Margot Fonteyn. They're ever so famous. You'll love it, honestly. They're brilliant."

"I bet I'll hate it."

"Bet you won't. Just watch for a bit. Go on, and then I'll put a film on, I promise. Just watch for a minute."

Tony didn't answer, but he didn't look happy. He looked more fed-up than I'd ever seen him.

The first dance was Rudolf Nureyev doing a piece from a ballet called *Le Corsair.*

"He's supposed to be a fierce pirate," I told Tony. He grunted. I said, "Stop grunting and just watch."

The music was a loud, leaping, brave sort of tune, and Nureyev jumped and turned so fast that he almost seemed to fly through the air.

"Just a few more minutes," I said, and looked over to make sure Tony wasn't too bored. He was leaning forward and staring at the screen.

"What's the matter?" I asked.

"Nothing," he said. "Can you rewind a bit and play this dance again?"

He made me play it again four times.

"You really like it, don't you?" I said.

"It's OK." He grinned at me. "Be even better to do it though. And I bet I could, too."

"Bet you couldn't. Loads of people think they can do ballet, but it takes years and years of training. Fantastically *hard* training. It's ever so difficult."

"It can't be that difficult." Tony stood up. "I'm going to try."

"You can't try here," I said. "You'll bump into the furniture."

He looked out of the window. "We could go into the garden. It's not raining any more."

"But it's still wet. Your feet'll get stuck in the mud, and your trainers'll get dirty."

"Then let's go into the road."

We live on a little cul-de-sac off a main road, so I knew we weren't going to be run over, but I said, "Won't you be embarrassed? Leaping about for everyone to see? They'll think you're mad."

"No, they won't," Tony said. "It's nearly tea-time. Nobody'll be looking. Come on, I want to try it."

We went out of the front door very quietly. I didn't want Tony making a fool of himself. He made sure there were no cars anywhere, and then stepped into the road. After that, he started copying what he'd seen Rudolf Nureyev doing on the video. I couldn't believe my eyes. He wasn't anything like Nureyev, of course, but he *did* seem able to jump very high, and his legs were straight and the most amazing thing was, he knew where to put his arms, and I could see that he was staring at the same spot each time he turned round (which is the proper ballet way to stop yourself from getting dizzy).

"There," he said when he'd danced back to where I was standing. "What do you think of that?"

"You're a cheat. You've had lessons," I said. "You must have done."

"I haven't."

"Really?"

"Really."

"Then you should," I said. "Come with me tomorrow. Miss Matting always say she's short of boys."

"You won't catch me in a ballet class," he said. "That's for girly wimps."

I was so furious I nearly kicked him, but I remembered my feet just in time. I yelled at him instead. "It's *not* for girly wimps! It's for brilliant, strong, athletic people. And if it *is* for girly wimps, then you're the biggest girly wimp of all, because you won't even try. *You're* too scared to even come to class. And you've got a gift for it. You could be dead good."

"What would I tell my friends? They'd think I was soppy, going and dancing round with a lot of girls."

"*I* think you're soppy for caring what a lot

of stupid boys think."

"Well, I *do* care, so there. I'm sorry, Louisa. Dancing's fun, but I'd hate going to class, OK?"

I took a deep breath. Tony was beginning to sound quite cross. I wasn't going to get

anywhere with him if I went on and on about Miss Matting's. An idea had just come into my head. I put on my kindest, best voice. "OK," I said. "You don't have to come to class if you don't want to, but what if I taught you some stuff? I could teach you all the things we do. How about that?"

"What sort of things?"

"Everything. We'll start with the five positions for the feet. You've got to know what they are. Come on."

"Can't I do some more jumping?"

"Tomorrow," I said. "We've got to begin at the beginning. Miss Matting says a good foundation is very important. Let's go to my house, because I've got the right music."

"Yes, Miss," said Tony, and followed me inside.

Chapter Three

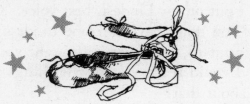

Tuesday is my best day of the week because I go to ballet straight after school. Tricia's mum picks me up in the car at four. I always get my suitcase ready on Monday night before I go to bed. Miss Matting says that real ballet dancers always make sure their ribbons are properly sewn on, and that their leotards and cardigans are clean. For the last couple of weeks, I'd enjoyed the lessons even more than I usually do, because as well as concentrating on my own dancing, I was also watching Miss Matting to see what real ballet teachers did, and trying very hard to remember all sorts of things which I could pass on to Tony at home.

He was a very good pupil. I never had to show him anything more than once. Miss Matting didn't tell us how good we were very often, but I told Tony all the time. I thought he'd like it. I also never stopped nagging him about coming to class with me, but nothing I said made any difference. I'd made him watch all kinds of videos, and he liked them a lot, and copied steps from them, but he wouldn't come to Miss Matting's with me, whatever I said to him.

Then one day in the car on the way to our ballet class, Tricia said, "Miss Matting's going to tell us something exciting today, do you remember? I can't wait to see what it's going to be. Maybe there'll be another show."

"No," I said. "She only does one a year. It won't be that."

"Here you are, girls," said Tricia's mum. "I'll pick you up at six."

We ran into the changing room. I love getting changed for class. I've never told anybody, not even Annie, what I pretend while I'm getting ready. I pretend I'm in Russia, at a proper ballet school, and that this class is for all the dancers in the corps de ballet of a real company. I pretend that Miss Matting isn't Miss Matting at all, but some very famous ballerina who's too old to go on stage and is passing on her knowledge to the next generation. I don't know many Russian names, so I think of my self as Louisa Posnansky. I'm sure Mrs Posnansky wouldn't mind if she knew, only of course she never will know, because I'll never tell anyone.

We always do exercises at the barre first. Miss Matting had a barre put up along one wall, but there's no mirror we can look into, so I usually imagine that as well. Some people don't concentrate on the barre exercises, but I always do, and today I was listening extra carefully to everything Miss Matting was saying, because I knew I'd have to go back and teach Tony all the things I'd learned.

"Back straight, Linda . . . Keep your toes pointed, really pointed, Alan . . . Jane, bend your knees, please, and lift, lift that arm . . . Grace and poise, Pamela, you're not about to throw a javelin, dear!"

After the barre exercises, we did more exercises in the middle of the room. I pretended I had blocked shoes on, and was going to do point work, even though I knew it would be years and years before I was really allowed to go up on my toes. It's only when your feet have grown strong that you can dance like that, and lots of girls don't understand this and try to go up on points much too early.

After the exercises were finished, we all sat on the floor. Miss Matting said, "Well, I

28

promised you a surprise last week, and now I'm ready to tell you about it. I think you're all ready to make up a little dance of your own. I want you to do it in pairs, please, and I'll ask to see your efforts in three weeks. So, find a partner and being to think about it. Please choose someone who can practise with you at home because, of course, there won't be time during class and in any case, I wish to be amazed by your performances. Making up the steps of a dance is called 'choreography', as I'm sure many of you know, so I want you all to become choreographers as well as dancers. Keep it simple and about three minutes long, please. It sounds like a very short time, but I promise you, once you start to plan your steps it'll turn out to be much longer than you think."

The moment Miss Matting started to tell us her surprise, I knew exactly what I was going to do. I'd make up a dance for me and Tony. In my head, I could see myself wearing a pale lilac tutu with roses in my hair, and Tony dressed in a blue velvet jacket. We weren't going to be dancing in costume, of course, but I couldn't help imagining it. I was going to dance with him and no one else.

"Will you be my partner?" Tricia asked.

"No, Weezer, be mine," Maisie begged.

"Louisa," I said, but I was so busy day-dreaming that I knew I didn't sound even a bit cross. "No, I'm sorry, Tricia, I'm really sorry, Maisie, but you two will have to do your dance together. I've got a secret partner."

"Who is it?" Maisie asked. "Is it Pam? Or Linda?"

"I'm not saying," I told her. "It wouldn't be a secret if I told you, would it?"

"I think you're a real meany," said Maisie, "not to tell us."

"It'll be a surprise," I grinned at her. "You'll see."

"Have you told anyone else?" Tricia asked.

"No," I said. "I might tell Annie. Or I might not. I'll decide later."

I did tell Annie. I told her all about it.

"But you must absolutely swear," I said, "not to tell a soul. Not a single, solitary soul."

Annie said, "OK, but I don't see how you can possibly get away without telling Tony what he's doing."

"If he knew he was going to have to dance at my ballet class, he'd never agree. So I'm just going to pretend a bit, that's all."

"He's sure to find out," said Annie.

"No, he won't," I smiled at her. "Not if you don't tell him. I'll think of a story for him, don't worry."

"And what about Tricia and Maisie? They're always coming round here to play, and they're bound to find out that you and Tony are dancing together."

"I've thought of that," I said. "I'll go and play at their houses for a bit, that's all. I won't

tell them any lies. I'll tell them they can't come round here because I'm preparing something special for Miss Matting, but that it's a deadly secret, and that's true."

"Won't they be hurt?" Annie asked.

"Why should they be?" My sister has some very funny ideas sometimes.

"Because they're your friends and friends aren't supposed to keep things secret from one another."

"It won't be secret for ever," I told her.

"Anyway, they know it's a dance I'm hiding from them, and not anything else."

"You're hiding Tony from them too," Annie said.

I sighed. "I'll tell them everything in the end," I said. "Don't worry about it."

Tony was getting better and better.

"I'm really pleased with you," I told him. "You're getting to be a proper dancer. I'm going to take you to meet Mrs Posnansky."

"Oh no, Weezer, please . . . I don't know her . . . I've only ever said hello to her once. Why do I have to go?"

"LOUISA!" I shouted. Then I said, "If you don't call me Louisa, I'll call you Ant." I knew Tony hated being called Ant because he'd told me so. I went on, "The reason we have to go is because I want her to see what a good dancer you are. I've told her all about you and all about our lessons. Also, I want to ask her advice about something . . . steps and stuff."

"What does she know about ballet?"

"She knows a lot. Her mum was a proper dancer in a real ballet company."

"I know," Tony said. "You showed me the headdress she wore in *Swan Lake* which Mrs Posnansky gave you . . . but I won't know what to say."

"I'll talk," I told him. "You won't have to say a thing."

Tony sighed. "Do I have to come?"

"Yes," I said. "You do. She always gives me chocolate. Sometimes she gives us cakes. And her house isn't like our house. It's different. You'll like it, you'll see. She won't eat you. She likes children."

"OK," said Tony. "I suppose I'll have to come or you'll never stop nagging me."

"That's right," I said. "I won't."

I knew the chocolate and cakes would persuade him. I think boys are greedier than girls.

Chapter Four

1 love going to Mrs Posnansky's. Her house is more like a house in a fairytale than any other place I've ever seen. All her furniture is made of dark wood, and there are velvet curtains at the windows. She has lots of framed photographs up on the walls of her lounge, and Annie and I love looking at them. Everyone in them is dressed in old-fashioned clothes and some of the men have very long moustaches and they're wearing big fur hats because it's very cold in Russia during the winter.

Mrs Posnansky took one look at Tony sitting rather uncomfortably on the sofa and said to him, "Today I have special cinnamon cake. This you like?"

"Oh, yes please," he said. "That sounds lovely."

"My Little Swan . . . she likes my cakes."

Tony looked a bit puzzled, so I explained.

"Mrs Posnansky means me. She always calls me that. I was in the Dance of the Little Swans, you see."

"It suits her," Mrs Posnansky said. "She is full of gracefulness and has long white neck, like a swan. Also, like swan, she loves to eat. When she comes, I have chocolate. You like too?"

"Oh, yes," said Tony. "I like chocolate. I like it a lot."

"You shall have," said Mrs Posnansky. "After the cake. I will go and bring."

"I'll help you," I told her, then I turned to Tony. "Just wait here," I said to him. "I'll be back in a minute."

While I was alone in the kitchen with Mrs Posnansky, I told her all about my plan to make up a dance with Tony as my partner.

"But he won't come to the ballet class with me," I told her, "so what can I say to him? How can I make sure he agrees to dance with me?"

Mrs Posnansky was pottering around, opening and shutting drawers, filling the kettle, and putting a plate full of slices of cake on to a trolley, together with some glasses for

the lemon
tea she always
gives her visitors.
"Tell him," she
said, "that there is a
show somewhere. How do you say it? A com-
petition to see who is best."

"You mean a talent contest?"

"I mean this . . . yes, my dear Little Swan.
A talent contest."

"What a clever person you are!" I said.
"Thank you."

"Not very clever," she said. "Only old. Now
you help to push this trolley in for me, please."

Tony became a lot chattier after he'd eaten the
cake, and by the time the chocolate came out,
he and Mrs Posnansky were the best of friends.

"I hear from my dear Little Swan," she said,

"that you are very strong dancer."

"Oh, well," Tony said blushing. "Weezer exaggerates a bit sometimes."

"Louisa," I hissed.

"Sorry, Louisa . . . Yes, I like dancing. And she's a good teacher."

"This I am sure of," Mrs Posnansky said, smiling. "I am sure she is of the strictest kind with no nonsense. This is for ballet the best sort of teacher. A soft teacher is not so good."

"She's not soft," Tony said. "She makes me practise every day."

"So," said Mrs Posnansky, "I wait eagerly to see you dancing together. You will be good partners, yes?"

"I don't know really," said Tony. "I haven't ever danced with her . . . not properly."

"Well," I said, taking a deep breath to get me ready for the

lie I was going to tell, "when we go home, we're going to start working out a dance to do together. There's a talent contest in a couple of weeks and I'd love to win it. Wouldn't you?"

"A talent contest?" Tony's eyes shone. "With prizes?"

I hadn't thought about that. I didn't want to promise prizes that we were never going to get so I just said, "I don't know what the prizes are," and then I began to talk about something else. After a while, I said, "We must go home now, Mrs Posnansky."

"Yes," said Tony. "I want to go and start working on our dance."

Mrs Posnansky walked slowly to the door with us, leaning on her stick. "Goodbye, Little Swan, and goodbye, Tony," she said. "Please come to show me your dance when it is ready."

"We will," I told her. "Thank you for having us."

"Yes, thank you," said Tony, and Mrs Posnansky said, "It is always a pleasure," and she waved at us as we crossed the road.

"Have you thought about what we're going to do?" Tony said as soon as we were in the lounge of my house.

"Not really," I said. "The dance has got to be about three minutes long. That sounds like a tiny amount of time, but it's long when you have to fill it up with steps."

"Well, I've been thinking," Tony said.

"When have you been thinking?"

"Ever since you told me about it across the road . . . anyway, listen. I reckon it'd be a good idea if we . . . well, it sounds stupid, but what if we danced a whole story?"

"In three minutes?" I laughed. "You're barmy, honestly."

"No hang on. You don't understand. I mean a really short story."

"How short?"

"What about a nursery rhyme?"

"A nursery rhyme? Are you mad? Nursery rhymes are for babies!"

"But everyone knows them, and if we do the one I'm thinking of, it will give us a chance to do some really brilliant things . . . really difficult steps, I mean. And there won't be that many people doing ballet in the talent contest, so at least we'll be different."

I gasped. I'd almost forgotten about the talent contest. I said quickly, "Which nursery rhyme were you thinking of? I don't fancy being Miss Muffet."

"What do you think of Jack and Jill? We could have fun working it out."

"Let's try it," I said. "Jack and Jill . . . right. Well. Come on, give me your hand and we'll start by walking up the hill."

We worked out the steps for going up the hill and Tony thought of a clever extra bit where we both started pulling on the handle of a pretend bucket. Then we worked out how we'd look down an imaginary well, and how we'd take turns winding the handle to bring up our bucket of water.

"The hardest bit," said Tony, "will be tumbling down the hill. We don't want to hurt ourselves by falling properly."

"I know," I said. "Can you do cartwheels?"

"Yes," said Tony, "but that's not real ballet, is it?"

I didn't know if it was or not, but I knew that cartwheels were fun to do and I was good at them, so I said, "It's modern ballet. We can have a sort of quarrel over who's going to be carrying the bucket down the hill and then I'll give you a push and you can go into two or three cartwheels. Let's try it."

"I can only do one cartwheel in here." Tony said.

"Never mind. Let's just see what it looks like."

Tony grabbed hold of an invisible bucket that was very heavy. We took turns to pull at it, and then I gave him a tap on the shoulder. He raised his arms above his head, and then spun into a perfect cartwheel, ending up on the carpet with his arms and legs bent into a funny shape and his face twisted in pretend pain. I clapped my hands.

"That's lovely," I said. "I'm going to do that, too. Watch!"

I did a cartwheel and tried to copy Tony as closely as I could. I ended up next to him, clutching my back.

"Yes," he said. "It's going to be great." He stood up. "Now . . . we must work on those steps at the beginning."

Chapter Five

Tony and I practised every day. We found a piece of music that fitted the Jack and Jill story really well. It was a march by Chopin, and whenever I heard it, it made me feel like striding out, up the hill. We rehearsed our cartwheels in the garden.

"Are you sure," Tony asked, "that the stage will be big enough for us to do three cartwheels?"

"Don't worry," I said, and started talking about something else. I couldn't tell him we wouldn't be on a stage, but would have the whole length of St Christopher's church hall to do our dance in.

On the Monday afternoon before the class, we went over to show Mrs Posnansky what we'd been rehearsing. She clapped her hands and said we were magnificent and splendid, and she gave us some chocolate to take home.

When we were back at my house, we ate all the chocolate, and then Tony said to me, "What are you going to do about your ballet class tomorrow? You're going to have to miss it, aren't you? To do this talent contest. Won't Miss Matting be cross?"

"Umm . . . " I hadn't thought about this. I said, "Oh, I've already told Miss Matting. She doesn't mind at all. Not just for this once. And I've told Tricia not to pick me up in the car tomorrow."

This was true. I'd said that Annie was bringing me because she wanted to see the dances that everyone had made up.

"What do you think we should wear?" Tony asked. "For Jack and Jill. We haven't thought of that."

I knew I was supposed to wear my tights and leotard to class, but I *did* want us to look as much like a brother and sister as possible, and I knew we both had red tracksuits. I could have my ballet stuff on underneath, and take the tracksuit off when the dances were finished and the proper class began. But what if the dances came last, after we'd done all the exercises? And what if Tony took one look at St Christopher's and saw that I'd tricked him? I'd told him the talent contest was being held in the sports centre. He'd go straight home. He'd probably never speak to me again. I was beginning to think that having Tony as my partner was not such a bright idea, but then I remembered what a good dancer he was, and I decided that I'd *make* him come into the hall with me, whatever he said.

On Tuesday afternoon, it didn't take Tony very long to work out that we weren't walking towards the sports centre.

"This isn't the way to the sports centre," he said. "Where are you going?"

"It's a short cut," I told him, hurrying along the pavement so that I wouldn't have to talk to him.

"No, it's not," he said, a bit breathlessly. "The centre's over there. I've lived here long enough to know that much."

I didn't bother to lie any more. I just muttered, "We're nearly there now," and Tony said, "Nearly where? Honestly, Weezer, you are a pain sometimes! Where are we going?"

"It's a surprise," I said, "and don't call me Weezer!"

"OK," he said. "But tell me the truth. This

talent contest isn't being held at the sports centre at all, is it? You didn't want to tell me because you thought I'd only come if it *was* at the sports centre. Right?"

"Right. Look, come on," I said. "It's getting late. We'll be there in a minute."

I was busy wishing St Christopher's wasn't such a big and churchy-looking church. There it was, right bang slap in the middle of town and everyone knew it.

As soon as Tony saw it, he cried, "But that's St Christopher's! That's where you go to ballet!"

I nodded. He went on, "You go to ballet on Tuesdays at four."

I nodded again. I felt like closing my eyes because I didn't like the way Tony's face had gone quite white. He was starting to look really angry.

"I know what you've done. You've brought me to your ballet class. That's horrible of you, Weezer, and I'm going to call you Weezer because you don't deserve to be a Louisa. I thought you were my friend, but you tricked me! Well, I'm not going to jump around in front of a whole lot of stupid girls. I'm going home."

He turned round and started walking down the road. I went racing after him. He couldn't go now, not after all our work. I shouted, "Tony! Stop, Tony! Stop and listen to me . . . Just listen for a second . . . please."

He stopped, and looked at me. He was still angry, but at least he seemed ready to listen.

"Tony, I'm sorry. I didn't like lying to you, but I had to do it, didn't I? When Miss Matting said we had to find someone to dance with, I just knew it had to be you because you're the best dancer I know. You're better than anyone else in my class . . . and I just thought we could do a really good dance."

I felt so sad when I thought that all our hard work had been for nothing that I started to cry. Tony came up to me and peered at my face.

"Don't cry. Please stop crying, Weezer. It's your own fault I won't come to your class. I said all along I wouldn't. Why are you crying?"

"I'm crying," I said, "because I've worked so hard and it's such a waste. You're a good dancer and you won't do anything about it. You worked hard too. *And* you enjoyed it, so don't say you didn't."

Tony sighed. He said, "All right, all right, I'll do it. I'll come into your class, just this once. Just stop crying, Weezer, please."

"OK," I said. "Thanks, Tony." I took my hankie out and blew my nose. I decided to ignore the Weezer. Tony was coming into my ballet class! I said, "It'll be fine, you'll see.

There *are* some boys in the class. I told you about them."

"Girly wimps!" he said, but he was smiling.

"No, they're not," I smiled back at him. "You'll see. They're ordinary boys like you. I'll take you in and introduce you to Miss Matting. I expect you'll have to wait to do our dance till we've done all our exercises."

Tony followed me into the hall. I'd made sure we were early, because I knew that I'd probably have to explain everything to Miss Matting.

"Hello, Louisa dear," she said, coming towards us as soon as she saw us come in. "Who is this young man?"

"It's Tony Delaney, Miss Matting."

"Hello, Tony," said Miss Matting.

"Hello," said Tony.

Nobody seemed to know what to do next, so I said, "Tony lives next door to me and we've made up a dance together."

"How delightful!" said Miss Matting. "I look forward to seeing it very much. You can sit on one of those chairs, Tony dear, just while we do our exercises."

Tony nodded and sat down. I ran to the

changing room to take off my red tracksuit. I'd have to put it on again for the Jack and Jill routine, but I didn't care. Tony was here. He was going to watch our class. He hadn't run away.

Tricia and Maisie were waiting for me in the changing room.

"It's Tony!" Tricia said. "He's your secret partner. Why didn't you tell us? We'd never have told anyone, honest!"

"Yes, but if I'd told you, then it wouldn't really have been a secret would it?" I said.

"I suppose not," said Maisie. "Is he a good dancer?"

"Wait and see," I said, and went into the hall to take my place at the barre.

Chapter Six

Tony and I had to wait until the very end of the class to do our dance. As soon as the exercises were over, Miss Matting said, "We'll have five minutes' rest everyone, and then I'll see your dances. I'm greatly looking forward to this, and I hope you are too."

I *was* looking forward to showing off our Jack and Jill dance, but while I was in the changing room getting into my tracksuit, I could feel my heart beating very hard in my chest. I went to sit next to Tony when I was ready, and I whispered to him, "I'm nervous. Are you?"

"No," said Tony. "Not really."

"Why not? Why aren't you?"

I couldn't understand Tony at all. He wasn't a bit like me. He never lost his temper – well, hardly ever – and now he was sitting here as calm as calm, not a bit worried about dancing in front of all these strangers.

I decided boys' minds just didn't work in the same way girls' minds did. I said, "Aren't you scared of forgetting the steps? Or falling over in the middle of a cartwheel?"

"Well," he said, "I know what we have to do. We've practised it enough, haven't we? We'll just do it the way we do it at home. I'm waiting to see what everyone else does. And guess what?"

"What?"

"I know James Williams."

"Really?"

"Yes, he goes to my school. He's in the class below me. I never knew he did ballet."

"He's not a silly boy," I said, "who thinks that only girly wimps do ballet."

"Ssh," said Tony. "They're starting."

Maisie and Tricia were the first pair to dance. They were pretending to be kittens. Linda and Pam were birds; two of the boys did a sailors' hornpipe. I watched each pair carefully, and they were all very good. I began to feel more and more nervous.

"No one's done a story yet," Tony whispered to me. "I think our dance is the best."

I thought that, too, only I'd never have said so to anyone except Annie. That doesn't really count, though, because she's my sister and I tell her everything.

Soon all the others had done their dances, and it was our turn.

"Louisa has brought a new boy to the class to be her partner, children," said Miss Matting. "Say hello to Tony Delaney, everyone."

Everyone said, "Hello Tony!" I thought he would be embarrassed, but he looked exactly the same as he always did, and he said "Hello," back to them.

I gave Miss Matting our music tape and she put it on for us. As soon as I heard the first chords, I forgot all about the others, and the room we were in, and Miss Matting. I even forgot about being the very best. I could almost see the steep hill in front of us, with the well at the top. When it came to pushing Jack, I held my breath for a moment, hoping that Tony wouldn't be put off his cartwheels by having to do them in a place he'd never even seen before, and on a surface he wasn't used to. I needn't have worried. He whirled along so fast that it really *did* look as though he were tumbling out of control, and when he landed at the bottom of the hill, the face he pulled as he clutched his sore head made the whole class laugh. They laughed again when I did my tumbling after, and when we'd finished, everyone clapped.

"Well," said Miss Matting, "I must say I'm very pleased with you all, class. You've worked very hard, and your dances were excellent, and I think Louisa and Tony were very clever to think of doing a whole story as a dance."

"It was Tony's idea," I said. "And he helped me with the choreography."

"It was a very good idea. Have you been going to ballet classes for long, Tony?"

"No, Miss Matting," he said.

"He's never been," I said. "I taught him all the positions and steps. I try to remember everything that you show us in class, and then I go home and teach it to Tony. He lives next door to me, so we can practise every day."

"Well, you're a very good teacher, Louisa. Maybe I'll take a holiday and leave you in charge."

"Oh no," I said. "I want to learn, Miss Matting. I don't want to teach."

"I was only joking, dear. Of course I shall go on teaching you all. But Tony, I would be very pleased if you joined the class. I think you've got a real gift and it would be a shame if you didn't develop it, don't you think?"

"Yes, Miss Matting, I suppose so," Tony said.

"So will you come every week? There's always a shortage of good male dancers, you know."

Tony looked at me and hesitated. I nodded at him. He turned back to Miss Matting and grinned at her. "OK. I mean, yes, I'd really like to come and learn properly. I'll ask my mum and dad tonight."

I was so happy that Tony was going to come to class with me every Tuesday that it wasn't until we were back at home and telling Annie all about it that I realised what he'd said to Miss Matting.

"You told Miss Matting you wanted to learn properly. Does that mean you think I don't teach you properly?"

"No, no, of course not," he said. "You've taught me brilliantly. Really you have. And I'm glad I'm coming to class with you on Tuesdays."

"Me and all the girly wimps," I said. "Don't forget them."

"I'm going home now," he said, "to ask my mum and dad, and tell them all about our dance."

He did some Nureyev-style leaps as he made his way to the front door and frightened poor Brad who was lying on the mat at the bottom of the stairs.

"Sorry, Brad," said Tony. "I didn't mean to scare you. 'Bye, Weezer."

"'Bye, Ant." I stuck my tongue out at him. "See you tomorrow."

That night in bed I said to Annie, "Miss Matting thinks Tony has a real gift. She said so."

"Well, you said so as well. Didn't you?"

"But I'm worried now," I said.

Annie groaned. "Honestly, you find things to worry about that no one else has ever thought of before. What is it now?"

"What if he's better than I am?" I said. "I don't mind him being gifted, but I want to be even more gifted."

"He's a boy," Annie said. "It's different. No one will be comparing him with you. And Margot Fonteyn had Rudolf Nureyev, didn't she? A real, proper ballerina needs a good partner. You told me that. You're always telling me that."

I closed my eyes and thought about this for a bit. I could see Tony and me taking a bow on a big stage with red velvet curtains behind us, just like Fonteyn and Nureyev.

"Blair and Delaney," I told Annie. "It has to be that way round — Louisa Blair and Tony Delaney — doesn't it?"

"Of course it does," said Annie. "It wouldn't be at all the same if his name came first. Now go to sleep, Weezer, it's late."

I was falling asleep as Annie was talking. I don't even know if she heard me saying, "Louisa . . . my name's Louisa," or if I was only thinking it in my head.

A Rival for Louisa

For Joanna Carey

Chapter One

Saturday is usually my best day of the whole week, because that's when I go to my special ballet class. I started going in the spring. Miss Matting spoke to Mum, and Mum phoned Dad. I made Mum tell me what Miss Matting had said to her.

"She said you had a gift for ballet, Weezer, and she wants you to go to her advanced class on Saturday mornings. Dad and I have agreed that you should."

That was one of the happiest days of my whole life, and I didn't even mind Mum calling me Weezer because I liked what she was saying so much.

There were ten of us in the special class. Then, a couple of months after I started, Miss Matting said she thought Tony should come too, so now we go together. It's very useful having him living next door. It means that we can both go over all the steps and routines, which makes them more fun. I don't mind a bit when Tony tells me what's wrong with something I'm doing, which is funny, because usually I hate being criticized. Miss Matting told me off about it once.

"Louisa," she said, "the greater your talent, the more critical I have to be. You do realize that, don't you?"

"Yes, Miss Matting," I said.

"Then we won't have you pulling sulky faces ever again, will we?"

"No, Miss Matting," I said. Was it possible that all the really great ballerinas never sulked? I didn't think so, not really. Still, I made up my mind to sulk less, and to keep my sulking hidden from Miss Matting if I ever felt like doing it during a class.

After that I was very good and well-behaved for ages, until today. I didn't exactly sulk today, but I was annoyed, and I kept on being annoyed even after I got home. My sister Annie noticed at once.

"What's the matter with you?" she asked.

"Nothing," I mumbled.

"Then why have you just thrown your precious ballet suitcase across the room like that?"

I flopped on to my bed and spoke into the pillow.

"I can't hear a word you're saying," Annie said at last. "Sit up and talk to me properly."

I did sit up in the end. "A new girl came to Miss Matting's today. She's come from another ballet class, on the other side of town, because everyone knows that our class is so good."

"Is that a reason for you to be so grumpy?"

"I am *not* grumpy!" I said. "I'm just annoyed."

"But why?"

"I told you. It's because of this new girl."

"What's the matter with her? Does she bite? Did she kick you? I don't understand, Weezer."

"LOUISA!" I hissed. Annie never seemed to learn. I wanted to be called by my proper name. A real Russian ballet dancer had told me it was romantic.

"Louisa," said Annie. "Sorry. Tell me about this girl. Is she ugly?"

"No, she's pretty. She has lovely brown hair with reddish bits in it. Not carroty red, but beautiful dark red."

"Where does she go to school?"

"Somewhere fancy, I expect. Her voice is dead posh. And you should see her car. It's huge, and it's so clean it shines."

"Your voice is quite posh," said Annie.

"Quite posh isn't the same as dead posh. She also says silly things in the changing-room, like 'oh my golly' and 'cripes'. Can you imagine any normal person saying 'cripes'?"

"Well, I wouldn't say it and you wouldn't, but it doesn't seem like a very good reason to dislike a person."

"That isn't why I dislike her," I said. "Though it doesn't make me like her any better."

"What is it then?"

"She's got a silly name."

"Tell me," said Annie.

"She's called Phoebe."

"I think that's a beautiful name."

"You don't! Not really. You can't . . . you just can't. It's a pathetic name."

"It's not pathetic. It's just old-fashioned," Annie said.

"Well, then it suits her. *She's* old-fashioned."

"How do you know?"

"I can tell," I said. "She was wearing a horrible pleated skirt. And shiny shoes. No one wears shoes like that any more. They're too babyish. We all wear trainers."

"That's still no reason not to like her. If you only liked people because of what they wore, then you wouldn't have any friends."

Annie is such a creep! I could feel myself getting cross with *her* now so I said, "I don't want to talk about it any more. It's boring. Talk about something else, Annie, for goodness' sake."

We went downstairs for supper and I forgot about Phoebe for a while. I remembered her again as I was trying to get to sleep. I thought about what I'd said to Annie. I hadn't told her the real reason I was annoyed. I didn't want to admit it, even to myself. It was because the new girl was a good dancer. She was definitely as good

as I was, and in the dark it was easier to think
something that made me feel really bad: maybe
she was even better. I know you aren't supposed
to mind about things like that, but I did. I just
couldn't help it. I wish, I said to myself, I wish,
wish, wish, that she would find another class to
go to somewhere else. I wish she'd just disappear.

Chapter Two

Phoebe didn't disappear. She came to the Saturday ballet class every week, and everyone else seemed to like her. She always chatted away as we got changed, and Eleanor and Michelle hung around her all the time. They said things like, "Oh, Phoebe, I really love your hairband!" or, "Where did you get that leotard?"

And she'd try to tell them, only she wasn't really much use because she'd say, "Gosh, I can't remember. I think my mother got it for me," or, "I honestly don't know."

I didn't mind other people being friends with her. I had best friends of my own: Tricia and Maisie, who didn't come to the Saturday class. I also had Tony to go and come back with, but all the same, Eleanor and Michelle and I used to be a kind of threesome. I suppose we could have become a foursome, but I still didn't like Phoebe.

She was always nice to me and this made me feel even worse. She wasn't a bit shy. If there was something she wanted to say, she just came right over to you and said it.

Also, she often asked me to show her things. One day she said, "Louisa, I really like the way you do pirouettes. Will you help me with mine?" So I showed her how I did them, and she copied me, and I corrected the way she was holding her arms, and after a while her pirouettes *were* looking much smoother.

"Thanks tons, Louisa," she said. That was a typically Phoebe-ish thing to say. No one else would ever use an expression like that. She smiled at me.

"I'm breathless now, and a bit dizzy. I'll never do them like you, of course, but I feel much happier with them now. You're a fantastically lively, sparkly kind of dancer. I'll never be as good as you."

I couldn't believe my ears. Did Phoebe *really* think I was 'fantastically lively and sparkly', or was she just saying so to try and get me to be a little more friendly? I liked her a bit better just for saying such a nice thing, and I knew I should have said something nice back to her, but I didn't. I just smiled and said, "Thanks, Phoebe."

I could hear Annie's voice in my head, saying, "Go on, Weezer, be a bit more friendly. It won't hurt you," but I didn't feel like being friendly, and I was a little ashamed of myself as I watched Phoebe walk over to the barre.

At the end of the class, Miss Matting said, "Go and change as quickly as possible, please, and then come and sit in here. I have some very exciting news for you all."

In the changing room everyone was giggling, wondering what the news would be.

"They want some kids for an advert," said Michelle.

"They're making a movie and need us for extras." That was Debbie.

"I bet it's a documentary about ballet schools," said Emma.

I didn't bother to wonder, but got changed as quickly as I could. We all did. Miss Matting laughed when she saw the whole class sitting quietly, waiting.

"Well," she said, "now I know how to get you all to hurry. I shall dangle exciting bits of news in front of you. But what I have to tell you now really *is* special. You've heard of the Sheridan Ballet Company, haven't you?"

We all nodded. The Sheridan was our local company.

"As you know, they always put on *The Nutcracker* at the Theatre Royal for the two weeks before Christmas, and with this particular ballet, they choose children from dance schools in the area to be in the production. Now I'm sure you're all familiar with *The Nutcracker* but for anyone who isn't, it has several parts for children. Dominic Sheridan himself is coming here next week to audition you all. He's looking for a dozen young dancers to be mice, I think, and four to be party guests and double up as children in the Land of Sweets in Act Two. You must remember, though, that other schools in the area are also being auditioned, so it's quite possible that none of you will be chosen. You must all be perfectly clear about that. Are you quite clear, Louisa dear?"

"Yes, Miss Matting," I said. Why did she ask me specially? I would have to talk to Tony about it on the way home. I couldn't wait to tell Annie. *The Nutcracker* was the very first ballet I ever saw and I'd watched the video hundreds of times. I must be chosen, I said to myself as we all stood up and made our way out of the hall. I must, must, must be chosen. Phoebe was right beside me as we left.

"I bet Mr Sheridan chooses you," she said to me, and she was actually smiling as she said it, almost as though she wouldn't have minded at all.

"No," I said, "I bet he chooses you," and I managed to smile as well. I even managed to say something nice. I said, "I think you really deserve to be chosen."

Annie would have been proud of me. I was proud of myself, and felt good all the way home, even though I was still anxious. How would I get through the next week, till the audition?

"I'm going to watch my *Nutcracker* video tonight," I told Tony. "Come and watch it too, if you like. Then we can see what we're going to be asked to do."

"Great!" said Tony. "Thanks."

He looked as though he couldn't care less about the audition. I didn't understand how anyone could be so easy-going.

Chapter Three

1 spent most of the next week when I wasn't in school or in bed practising for the audition. Annie and Mum got quite sick of me pretending to be a mouse.

"Stop nibbling your toast like that," Mum said. "You look ridiculous."

"She's still being a mouse," Annie explained.

"I know she's being a mouse, but I don't remember any toast-nibbling scenes in *Nutcracker*," said Mum. "I think all the mice do is have a fight, and rush around the stage waving swords, and swishing their tails about. The King Mouse has a slipper thrown at him. I do remember that."

"I'm being in character," I explained. My mum doesn't understand about character. "If you're a mouse, then everything you do has to be mouse-like."

"Doesn't this Mr Sheridan want some nice, well-behaved children to go to a Christmas party at the beginning of Act One?" Annie asked. "You could practise being a well-behaved child."

"I'll never be chosen as one of those," I said. "My only chance is to be the best and most mouse-like mouse in the world. Phoebe will probably be a party child . . . it would suit her. She always looks as if she's just off to some posh do or other."

"Well, just for now," said Mum, "please sit normally on your chair and eat your breakfast like a human being."

"I'm glad I don't have to walk to school with you any more," Annie said. She had started going to Fairvale High in September, so now I walked to school with Tony.

"That's not a very nice thing to say," said Mum. "Poor old Weezer, she's not that bad, is she?"

"Not usually," said Annie, "only I saw her and Tony going off yesterday, and they looked really mad. What were you doing, Weezer?"

"Louisa," I said. "We were scampering. Mice scamper, in case you didn't know."

"I think," said Annie, "that we should call you 'Cheezer' from now on."

I threw my piece of toast at her, and it missed
her and hit poor Brad, our cat, who was curled up
on the kitchen chair.

"Stop it, girls," said Mum. "Go and get ready
for school, both of you. I don't want any more of
this silly mouse nonsense. Goodness knows what
will happen if you *do* get the part, Louisa. We'll
have to put up with you being a full-time
mouse."

"It's OK," I said. "There's not much chance, really. Miss Matting said so." But even as I said it, I was crossing my fingers under the table, just for luck.

There was about half an hour after I got back from school before Annie arrived. Usually, I went to Tony's house, but today I decided to go and visit Mrs Posnansky. She is always a good person to talk to if you are worried. She never laughs at me, and she never thinks I am silly to care so much about ballet. That is because her mother was a real ballerina, years and years ago, and Mrs Posnansky truly believed me when I said I was going to be a ballet dancer too. I like her house. It is dark and quiet and she always gives her guests lovely cakes and biscuits.

"Come, Little Swan," she said when she saw me at the door. "Is tomorrow the big audition? You must be nervous. Come and eat and drink and you will feel better."

I don't mind Mrs Posnansky calling me Little Swan. In my extra-special treasures box, I keep the headdress her mother wore when she was in *Swan Lake* and which she gave me for my first dancing display.

"Now tell everything," she said, as I drank

my tea and ate a brandy snap. "Is a mouse you wish to be? In *The Nutcracker*?"

"I don't mind what I am," I said, and in a way it was true. "Imagine! We'd be in a real theatre, performing for two weeks. We'd be with all the grown-up dancers. Would they talk to us, do you think?"

"From time to time, yes, I think," Mrs Posnansky said. "But if you are not chosen, my dear . . . what will happen? You will be sad."

"I know. I try to get ready for not being chosen. I lie in bed and say to myself, Louisa, you are not going to be a mouse. You will be very sad, but it doesn't matter, because you will have tried your best, and there will be other chances."

"How sensible you are, Little Swan! I am admiring this very much," said Mrs Posnansky.

"But it's not true," I told her, and took another brandy snap.

"How, not true?"

"I *will* care, and I *will* be sad, and I won't even think for a minute about other times. I want to be chosen *this* time. I wouldn't tell anyone but you. And Annie."

Mrs Posnansky sighed. "The dancer's life is hard and filled with disappointment. This I know. Is hard that this sadness must begin when you are so young."

I munched in silence for a while, and then I said, "May I tell you something? I haven't told this to anyone else at all, not even to Annie. Do you promise not to tell anybody?

"Of course," said Mrs Posnansky. "You trust me."

"I'm going to be a bit disappointed even if I am a mouse. What I really want to be is a party child. Isn't that awful?"

"But why do you wish to be a party child?"

"Because the party children have a dance in the First Act and pretty clothes, and they get to be in the Land of Sweets as well. All the mice do is rush about in a great gang and they wear furry grey costumes that aren't a bit pretty. So that's what I'd really love, only that'll never happen, so I'm hoping to be a mouse. That's second best, but it's still good."

"I wish for you," said Mrs Posnansky. "Come and tell me the news. If it is bad, we take out the chocolate to cheer us up. If it is good we take out the chocolate to rejoice."

"You mean to celebrate," I said.

"Yes, yes," said Mrs Posnansky. "To celebrate."

On Saturday, the changing-room was very quiet. Nobody felt like talking. We all knew that today was going to be a very special lesson.

"I saw him," Eleanor said. "I saw Mr Sheridan arriving. He's in there with Miss Matting."

"How do you know it's him?" Emma asked.

"I've seen his picture in the paper," said Eleanor. "And he lookes just like a dancer. All in black with a walking stick."

We went into the hall, and there he was, just as Eleanor had described him. He was sitting very upright on a chair, and Miss Matting was standing next to him. He was very handsome, even though he looked quite old.

"Good morning, children," said Miss Matting. "This is Dominic Sheridan. I know you all know who he is. He's come to look at you this morning because he needs young dancers for *The Nutcracker*, and I'll let him tell you himself what he wants you to do."

Mr Sheridan stood up, and Miss Matting sat down.

"Greetings, children," he said. "I want you all to pretend that I'm not here."

We all looked puzzled. How could we possibly pretend that?

He went on. "I'm not going to ask you to do any special routines, or steps. I am simply going to watch you have your class as normal. I shall walk about and look at you more closely, and I just want to see you doing the things you always do. Now, I'm sure you all start with the barre exercises, so line up there and we'll begin."

All the time I was doing my barre exercises, I felt cross. I'd been being a mouse all week for nothing. Now Mr Sheridan would never see how truly mouse-like I could be. I went through my pliés and demi-pliés, and out of the corner of my eye I could see Mr Sheridan looking at a piece of paper on a clipboard.

"I bet," whispered Phoebe, who was standing behind me, "that that's a list of our names. Can you see what Miss Matting is doing?"

I shook my head, no.

"I can," said Phoebe. "She's looking over here at us and then pointing. She's telling him what we're all called. That's what I think."

She sounded breathless and I could hardly hear her because she was whispering very quietly. When we turned round with our other hands on the barre, I was behind her, and I whispered to her:

"Are you nervous?" and she nodded her head, yes.

The class seemed to go on for ever. At last it was over.

"Thank you, children," said Mr Sheridan. "You are all a credit to Miss Matting. I'm sorry you can't all be in *The Nutcracker* but I do hope everyone will come and see the show, and support the people whom I have chosen. Let's see . . . where is that list?"

Miss Matting gave him the clipboard, and he smiled at us. I was finding it very hard to breathe, and I could feel my face burning. I looked at Phoebe, and she smiled at me and held up her hand with the fingers crossed. How could she be so friendly at a time like this? Tony was staring out of the window and didn't even seem to be paying attention. How could he be so calm? Perhaps there was something wrong with me for caring so much.

"Mice first, I think," said Mr Sheridan. "Here we are: Tony Delaney, Colin Shand and Phoebe Winters."

I could feel myself wanting to cry. I'm not a mouse, I thought. They haven't chosen me. I'm not a mouse.

"And now, party children. Well, I'm afraid we only need a very few of these, so only one name here: Louisa Blair."

"Me?" I think I said. I can't really remember, because all of a sudden everyone was crowding round me, and Phoebe was hugging me. I remember that.

"Oh, Louisa," she said. "It's us! It's both of us!

31

We're going to be in *The Nutcracker*. Really and truly! And Tony and Colin. Isn't it wonderful? It's the most delicious thing that's ever happened! Isn't it? Isn't it?"

I hugged Phoebe back. I couldn't help it, I was so happy. And I decided in that second, I liked her. I really did. There was nothing wrong with her. She was nice. And even though she didn't seem to know what 'delicious' meant, she was the only person who never, ever called me Weezer.

Chapter Four

All the rehearsals for *The Nutcracker* were being held in the studio which Mr Sheridan's company always used. This was at the back of a small theatre called The Playhouse, which was so far away from where we lived that Tony and I had to go on the bus.

"Are you sure," Mum asked the first time we had to go, "that you'll be all right? Will you know where to get off? And will you make sure you don't lose your fare money?"

I sighed. I was just about to moan at her for thinking we were babies, when Tony said, "Yes, we'll be fine, Mrs Blair. I'll look after Louisa."

"I can look after myself, thank you very much," I said and kicked him under the table. "Or maybe I'll have to look after you. You're always in a dream."

"I am not!" said Tony. "Anyway, we should go

or we're going to be late."

We weren't late. We'd set out so early that we were almost the very first people there. We waited for Phoebe to arrive. When she did, Tony and I waved at her, and after she'd got out of the car, she said, "Did you come by bus? That's silly. You must come with me in the car. We'll come and collect you next time. OK?"

"OK," I said. "Thanks, Phoebe."

"Yes, thanks," said Tony. "I'd love to ride in that car."

"Cripes!" said Phoebe. "This is it. Shall we go in?"

We went in, and a kind lady who was sitting knitting just inside the door said, "Hello, my darlings . . . you must be some of the mice, I expect. I think Mr Sheridan said you were to wait in the big rehearsal room. It's over there."

Other children began to arrive soon after. There were ten other mice, and a boy called Michael was my partner as a party child. Phoebe, Tony and I sat on a bench together. Dancers, real grown-up dancers, began to arrive, dressed in all sorts of strange things: torn sweatshirts, tatty leg-warmers, and ropey-looking scarves. The ladies all had huge shoulder bags, and their hair was scrunched up in ponytails. They didn't look in the least glamorous. One of them came up to us.

"Hi!" she said. "I'm Clara. I mean, my real name is Nikki, but I'm dancing Clara. Are you mice?"

"I'm not," I said. "I'm a party child. They're mice, though."

"It's going to be ever such fun," said Phoebe,

when Nikki had wandered away.

Mr Sheridan clapped his hands then, and we all had to go and stand in the middle of the room, while he explained what he wanted. Clara and the Nutcracker were going to dance first, and then we would do our bits. We sat on the bench and watched.

"He's not a bit like he was when he came to see us," Phoebe whispered. "He's shouting at them. Listen. Do you think he'll shout at us?"

Mr Sheridan *did* seem very cross.

"Nikki, darling, are you an elephant? Have you no idea of grace? What has happened to your arms? You are a young girl, not a shop-window dummy, sweetheart. Again, please."

"He says 'Again, please' so much . . . Do you think he'll be cross when it's our turn? I'm a bit scared," Phoebe said.

I was a little scared too, but I knew that famous choreographers often shouted at their dancers.

"He doesn't mean it," I said. "He just wants her to do her best. Anyway, I'm sure he won't shout so much at us. He hardly knows us."

When Clara and the Nutcracker came over to the bench, I could see that they were very sweaty. Nikki took a towel out of her bag.

"Your turn now, kids," she said to us. "He's a real slavedriver, but his bark is worse than his bite. Not much worse, but worse."

When it was the turn of the mice to do their steps, Mr Sheridan *did* yell at them.

"They're doing their best," I said to Nikki. "Why isn't he pleased with them?"

"Oh, Sherry never shows us when he's pleased. He reckons we only do well when we're terrified. Take no notice of him, that's my advice."

Tony and Phoebe looked a lot less terrified than the other mice. They went through the routine three times, and then it was the turn of the party children. We were going to do the scene in Act One, where everyone arrives for the Christmas party. There were four of us, and seven grown-ups.

"Michael and Louisa hold hands . . . Three skipping steps to the right, please . . . No, no, no, are you deaf, children? *Right*, not left. Really, what good are you to me as dancers if you don't know your right from your left?"

I couldn't help what happened next. I know you aren't meant to answer back, or argue during a ballet class, or a rehearsal. I know real dancers have to do exactly what they are told, but I lost my temper. Phoebe says I stamped my foot, but I can't remember that.

I do remember saying, "I *do* know my right from my left, Mr Sheridan, but it's hard to think properly when you shout at us. We're just getting a bit mixed up, that's all. It's the first time we've done this routine."

As soon as the words were out of my mouth, I felt sure Mr Sheridan would throw me out of the rehearsal, but everyone laughed and clapped, and he bowed to me and said, "Out of the mouths of babes, dear child . . . I am a brute and a beast, and apologize. Nevertheless, I shall continue to shout at you. I can't change the habit of a lifetime, I'm afraid. I mean no harm, I assure you. Take no notice of the volume of my

remarks, just do what I tell you to, and all will be for the best. Now. Take Michael's hand, and skip to the right. Yes, like that. Good."

"And then," Phoebe said to Annie, "Louisa said, 'It's the first time we've ever done this dance,' and Mr Sheridan apologized. He actually apologized! Nobody could believe their ears."

We were sitting at the kitchen table in my

house. Phoebe's mother had given Tony and me a lift home, and arranged with our parents to pick us up and bring us back every time there was a rehearsal.

"That's extremely kind of you," my mother said. "Would Phoebe like to stay to tea? We'd love to have her."

"It's Friday, Mum," I said. "Could Phoebe stay the night? Then we can go to the Saturday class together tomorrow morning."

I said the words before I'd really thought, but as soon as our mums had agreed that it would be all right, and that yes, Phoebe could borrow some pyjamas, I felt really happy. I thought, I'll show her all my ballet stuff after tea. I couldn't wait for her to see my Little Swan headdress.

Chapter Five

"Being in *The Nutcracker*," Phoebe said to me as we watched Mr Sheridan shouting at the Sugar Plum Fairy, "is the most fun I've ever had."

I nodded. "I love these rehearsals. And next week we'll actually be in the theatre. We're trying on our costumes on Thursday."

Phoebe wrinkled her nose. "Yours will be nicer than mine. I'll be so hot in a mouse suit, and you'll probably have a lovely dress. I'm dead jealous."

One of the Snowflakes, the one Phoebe and I didn't like much, frowned at us. Whispering while the principals were working was not allowed. We pulled silly faces at her back when she turned away, but we *did* shut up. I thought about how strange it was that I liked Phoebe so much now. I'd tried to explain to Annie yesterday. Phoebe, I told her, was funny, and always let me look at her programme collection whenever I went round to see her. When I slept over at her house, she let me sleep on the top bunk even though I knew she liked it best. She never got bored with watching ballet videos, or talking about all the dancers.

But best of all, she really liked me. She told me all her secrets, and she said she enjoyed coming to our house because, as she put it, "You've got both the things I want most in the whole world: a sister and a cat. My mum says it's too late for a sister, and she's allergic to cats."

"I don't mind if you share Brad and Annie," I said, and we giggled. I hadn't said anything particularly funny, but that was just Phoebe. She giggled about all sorts of things. During *Nutcracker* rehearsals, Mr Sheridan called her Minnie, which I thought was a bit silly, but it made her laugh each time he said it. He called me Madam, and I didn't know whether he was being rude or polite, but he always smiled when he said it so I didn't mind too much. All the grown-ups made a fuss of us. Tony had more peppermints given to him than he could eat. The Nutcracker Prince shared his ginger biscuits with us, and the corps de ballet ladies let us listen to them while they gossiped. They also gave us nearly-finished lipsticks, and powder puffs they didn't like any more, so we started building up a make-up collection in a shoe-box.

A week before the first night, the snow fell.

"This makes everything really Christmassy," said Phoebe. "I love the snow."

"It's OK," I said, "but it turns to slush and then ice and you can't play snowballs any more. And it's cold. And it makes your gloves wet. And your shoes."

"Don't be a misery, Weezer," said Phoebe. Now that Phoebe came to our house so much and heard Annie calling me that, she'd started, and when I shouted at her, she didn't do what everyone else did and apologize at once. She said:

"You ought to be pleased that I'm calling you by your affectionate diminutive. It shows how much I like you."

"Affectionate *what*?"

"Diminutive. You know . . . like a pet name. Affectionate diminutive is what my dad says it is when he calls me Beebs."

"Beebs? That's worse than Weezer. Poor old you! Well, I shan't call you that."

"You can if you like. I don't care."

"Well, I care. I hate my whatever-it-was-you-called-it, so I'm not using yours."

One of the things Phoebe and I liked doing best of all was watching the grown-ups rehearsing.

"I can do that bit," I said to her, as we watched the Sugar Plum Fairy from the wings. "Look at me!"

I started copying the steps. I'd been practising them at home and, apart from not being up on points, I thought I did it perfectly. Then I took a step sideways and stumbled. There were always pieces of furniture backstage and bits of the set as well. But I thought I knew exactly where they were. I forgot that a foot stool had just been put back after the party scene and I tripped over it in the middle of my dance. I clutched at a chair, but my feet just seemed to slip from under me, and I fell into a heap on the floor. My foot felt as if someone had bashed it very hard with a iron bar, and I started shrieking and crying, and all I could do was lie there. Everyone came running to see what all the noise was, and in the end I was sent home in a taxi with one of the ladies from the corps to keep me company.

"I want to go with her!" Phoebe cried. "Please let me go with Weezer. She's my friend." Even in the middle of my pain, this made me

feel a bit better, but Mr Sheridan was rehearsing the mice, and didn't let her come. I looked out of the back window of the taxi as it drove off, and there was Phoebe waving and weeping, wiping the tears away with the back of her hand.

The doctor came. Annie and my mum were just standing there looking worried while he poked and prodded at my foot. He arranged for me to go and have an X-ray, and then he bandaged it very tight, and told me not to walk on it.

"What about dancing?" I said. "I'm in *The Nutcracker*. At the Theatre Royal. It starts next week. Will I be OK next week?"

"Dancing?" The doctor shook his head. "You won't be dancing on this foot for at least three weeks."

"But . . . the show will be finished in three weeks! It's Christmas in three weeks. How can I just lie here while they're dancing in the theatre? What about my dance? I've got a dance with Michael. I'm in the Christmas party scene."

"Don't shout at the poor doctor, Louisa," my Mum said. "It's not his fault you've hurt your foot. I'm really so sorry, sweetheart. I know that dancing in *The Nutcracker* means a lot to you, but it would be silly to dance on that foot. You don't want to injure yourself in such a way that you couldn't dance when you were older, would you? I'm dreadfully sorry."

I started howling, "Being sorry isn't any good! I don't care how sorry everyone is! I just want to dance. I'm never going to cheer up. Never. I don't care how hard you all try to make me feel better. I won't. So there. I shall feel miserable *for ever*."

Annie looked so upset that I felt a bit sorry for her, but I was just too sad to say anything. This is the very worst thing that has ever happened to me, I said to myself, and it's all my fault. If only I'd been a bit more careful. It was horrible not to have someone else to be cross with. I wished I could just go to sleep and not have to talk to anyone. Brad was curled up next to me on the sofa and I picked him up and plonked him on my lap. I knew he wouldn't say anything.

Phoebe came to see me the next day. I was still sulking when she came in, but I stopped when I saw her. She looked as if she'd been crying for hours.

"Oh, Weezer," she said. "I've been crying for hours."

"I know you have. Your eyes are all red."

"I don't care. It's just so awful. It's the most awful thing I can think of!"

"You're the only one who thinks that. Apart from me of course. Everyone else tells me to cheer up and it could have been worse. They don't understand. You do. You know how I feel."

Phoebe started crying all over again. "I don't know how to tell you this, Weezer, so I'm just going to tell you. OK?"

Whatever did she mean? What was she going to tell me?

"Go on," I said. "What is it, Phoebe? What's the matter?"

"It's me. I'm the one Mr Sheridan has chosen. To do your dance with Michael in the party scene, and . . ." Phoebe could hardly speak she was crying so much. "The dress is beautiful. It's the most beautiful dress I've ever seen and you can't wear it. I feel so bad. I wish you could be in it. I do really. Do you believe me?"

"Of course I do," I said. I felt as if a huge stone was suddenly pressing on my stomach. I felt sick. I felt so jealous of Phoebe that I could hardly breathe, but she was crying so much, and she was so sad for me that I couldn't be cross with her.

"Don't cry, Phoebe," I said. "Really. I know that someone has to do my dance, and I'm glad

it's you. Really. You'll be brilliant. I know you will."

Phoebe flung her arms around me and hugged me. "I won't be as good as you, Weezer. No one could ever be as good as you."

I started crying then, all over again. *That* was why Phoebe was such a good friend. She always seemed to say exactly the right thing.

Chapter Six

"You will come to the show, won't you, Weezer?" Phoebe asked. She had come to see me every day since my fall, and she'd told me all *The Nutcracker* news. "Everyone wants you to come, and Mr Sheridan says he told you you could have a box for the first night. You *must* come."

Everyone had been extra specially nice to me. The day after my fall, a huge bunch of flowers arrived and a card signed by every single member of the company. We didn't have enough vases, and we had to borrow from Tony's mum and from Mrs Posnansky. She brought chocolate, and a beautiful fluffy muff, made of something that looked just like proper fur. She told me all sorts of stories about her mother, and terrible things that had happened to her while she was a dancer.

"You remember, Little Swan, to learn from the bad things. This makes you strong."

"I don't mind not being strong," I said, "as long as I can dance. That's all I care about."

"But to dance you have to be very strong. Not just in the body, also in the head."

As the days went on, I did get a bit stronger in the head, but I was still sad. I didn't know whether going to see the show was going to make me feel better or worse. I was curious, though. I wanted to see Tony being a mouse, I wanted to see the dress I might have been wearing, and I *really* wanted to see how Phoebe danced my steps. I was getting very good with my crutches, too, and I'd been going to school every day in Tony's mum's car.

"OK," I said to Phoebe. "I will come."

"Brilliant!" said Phoebe. "My mum says she'll come and pick you up, and Annie and your mum, and Mrs Posnansky. The box is huge. Everyone will fit. And you must come backstage afterwards and see me. I told them you would. You will, won't you?"

"Oh, yes," I said. "I really miss everyone, even shouty old Mr Sheridan. I'm going to wear my best dress, and my new muff. I can't wait now."

"Nor me," said Phoebe. "Do you know, Mr Sheridan is always telling me how dreadful I am, and how unfortunate it was that that you fell over!"

"He doesn't mean it," I said. "He's just saying that."

But I couldn't help thinking about what Phoebe had said, and wondering if Mr Sheridan really *did* mean it.

I'd never sat in such a grand place to watch a ballet before. The seats were covered in red velvet and the curtains at the back of the box were also red, and matched the stage curtains. Mrs Posnansky had brought a fan in case we felt hot, and a pair of tiny little binoculars which she said were called opera glasses, even if you were watching ballet or a play. Annie and I had fun before the show started, looking at people in the stalls who didn't know we were watching them.

"Look at her hair," said Annie. "It's coming down at the back. Do you think she knows?"

"I can see Miss Matting over there!" I said when it was my turn to look through the glasses. "And Eleanor and her mother. If we wave, do you think they'll notice us?"

"You can't behave like that in a box," said Mum. "You have to be very lady-like in a box. And in any case, here's the orchestra. The lights will go down in a minute. Just sit quietly, please."

For once, I didn't mind doing what my mother told me to. I could imagine what Phoebe was feeling, backstage. I could imagine the butterflies in her stomach, and how dry her mouth must be. I listened to the music. Then the curtains parted and there was Fritz and Clara's house, and the Christmas tree in the corner, and there was Nikki, in a white dress with a blue sash, doing exactly the same steps I'd

seen her do many times, only because she was
dancing under lights and in costume on a proper
set, they didn't seem like steps any more, and
then she stopped being Nikki, and became Clara.
I heard my cue, the notes I always waited for
before my entrance, and there she was, Phoebe, in
a dress made of gorgeous, rustly, shiny taffeta,
which was magic, because it looked green
sometimes and red sometimes. It depended on
whether the light was shining on it, or not.
Phoebe and Michael did my dance, and I almost
forgot that it *was* my dance. Phoebe did it
beautifully. I felt happy and sad at the same time.
I was happy for Phoebe, and sad for me.

In the interval, I tried to explain my feelings
to Mrs Posnansky and Annie.

"I just wish it was me, that's all. I'll never
know if I could have been as good as Phoebe, so
I'm sad. But I'm happy that she's so good,
because that makes the whole ballet good."

"This is natural," said Mrs Posnansky. "And
your friend is good dancer, but she is not dancer
like you. You have different style. She is quieter.
She is more dignified. You are . . . you are lively.
Sparkling. You are like quicksilver, she is like
silk . . . slow and smooth."

I looked at Mrs Posnansky in amazement.

"That's what Phoebe said about my dancing. How did you know?"

"She said this? She is clever, then, as well as good dancer. I will come backstage with you to congratulate."

"Oh, yes," I said. "She'd love that. And I'm dying to see the rest of the ballet, aren't you?"

"Yes," said Mrs Posnansky. "Come, we will return to our box."

All four of us went backstage after the show. It took us a long time, because of my crutches, but I didn't mind. Half of me was still in the magical land where snowflakes danced, and Christmas presents came to life and took you to the Land of Sweets, home of the Sugar Plum Fairy who welcomed everyone to a place full of wonders, like flowers who could leap across the stage.

"Louisa!"

"Precious child!"

"Darling . . . you poor brave little thing, you!"

"Louisa, how divine to see you, pet!"

All sorts of people stopped us on the way to the big dressing-room where the mice and the children were changing. I hadn't thought that some of them even knew my name.

Mr Sheridan was standing in the corridor outside Nikki's dressing-room, and he bowed to me, and said, "My dear, I'm so sorry you had to miss this chance. Little Minnie Mouse did well, didn't she?"

"Yes," I said. "But I wish it could have been me. And thank you for sending those lovely flowers."

"We were all so sad for you, my little Madam! But you never know, there is always next year, isn't there?" He tapped the side of his nose with his finger, which was a very un-Sheridan-like thing to do.

"What do you think he meant?" I asked Annie.

"I think he'll let you do your dance next year."

"Really? You mean I'll get another chance?"

"I don't see why not. You said he puts on *Nutcracker* every year."

Suddenly, I felt perfectly happy. I went into the big dressing-room, where Phoebe and Tony were already in their own clothes.

"You were ever so good," I told him. "But you look funny. You've still got your whiskers on."

"They aren't whiskers," Tony said. "That's my mouse-tache. Ha ha!"

"That's a really pathetic joke, Tony," I said, but I giggled as well.

Phoebe ran over to me from the other side of the room. "Weezer! You're here! Hello, everyone!"

"You were lovely," I said. "You really, really were. And you looked great in my dress."

"It isn't your dress. It's *our* dress. You can have it another time."

"Yes," I said, "and we can both be famous at the same time. Mrs Posnansky explained to me that there are different kinds of dancers. She said we were like quicksilver and silk."

"Like Darcey Bussell and Viviana Durante."

"Exactly," I said. "We can do different parts. I'll do Coppélia."

"I'll do Giselle," Phoebe said.

"What about *Swan Lake*? I said. "I want to do that."

"So do I," said Phoebe. "Maybe we can take turns to do Odette and Odile. Louisa and Phoebe . . . Phoebe and Louisa. Doesn't that sound great, Weezer?"

"Yes, Pheezer. I think it sounds terrific."

"Pheezer?" Phoebe said. "What's that when it's at home?"

"It's your new affection-whatsit . . . dim-something."

Pheezer giggled. "I like it. Pheezer and Weezer."

"No," I said. "You've got it the wrong way round. Weezer and Pheezer."

Louisa in the Wings

For June and John Crebbin

Chapter One

Mum said, "Louisa Blair, I just despair!" and I said, "You're a poet and you don't know it!"

"Annie," Mum turned to me, "you're not exactly helping. I thought you might have tried to explain to Weezer why it is I can't do what she wants me to do."

"Louisa," said Weezer. "I keep telling you to call me that and you never do, so I don't see why I should listen to what you're trying to tell me."

"I *did* call you Louisa." Mum was beginning to sound harassed. "If you remember, I said it a couple of seconds ago. I even, according to Annie, turned it into a poem, so a little less of your nagging would be greatly appreciated."

"I'm not nagging," said Weezer, but of course she was. Nagging is as natural to my little sister as breathing. She has just turned eight, and seems to be getting better and better at it. I know her very well so I could imagine exactly what she was thinking. It must have been something like, "Well, being cross hasn't got me my way, so I'll try being sweet and see what Mum says," because suddenly her face was all smiley and her voice wasn't a bit whiney.

She said, "Mum, please explain why I can't go to the ballet. I promise I won't ask you again, but I just want to remind you that this will be a really wonderful chance to see almost my very favourite ballet, *Coppélia*, and it's danced by a company that comes all the way from St Petersburg. That's in Russia, and Russians are top champion dancers. That's what Mrs Posnansky told me, so it must be true."

Mum sat down next to Weezer and spoke gently. "I know all this, Louisa. Mrs Posnansky is quite right, and it *is* a wonderful company. I've never said you can't go. All I've said is, I cannot afford twenty pounds for each ticket. I couldn't let you go alone, so Annie would have to go with you, and that's forty pounds. I just can't manage it at such short notice."

"Why not?"

"Lots of reasons." Mum began to tick them off on her fingers. "Firstly, I've just paid the deposit on our summer holidays. Secondly, you're going to ballet classes twice a week now, as you wanted. Thirdly, Annie needs a whole new school uniform when she goes to Fairvale High in September, and fourthly, you used up all your savings on your new bike."

"What about Dad?" Weezer asked. "If I write and ask him, won't he send me the money?"

"Dad helps us as much as he can as it is. He has to think about his new house and family."

"I don't see why." Weezer stuck her bottom lip out and sniffed. "We came first, before his new family. He should think of us."

"He *does* think of us," I said. "He's always sending us things, and he pays for the tickets when we go and visit him, doesn't he?"

"Anyway," Mum said, "you're making me sound like some kind of ogre, who'd want to stop you going to see *Coppélia*. That's simply not true. I've said I'd pay for two gallery seats – they're only four pounds each. I really don't see why you're not happy with that."

"Because," Weezer said patiently, "sitting in the gallery is no good at all. You might as well look at the ballet on a video in the next room. All the dancers will be tiny, and I won't be able to see their feet properly or the expressions on their faces. I'd rather not go at all than have to sit in the gallery."

"Then it's not going at all, I'm afraid," Mum said. "Now come on, both of you. Help me wash up the supper dishes and then, Annie, you must go and do your homework."

"I haven't got any," I told her. "It's half-term next week, don't you remember?"

"What with your sister filling my head all afternoon, I'm quite surprised that I can remember my own name."

"I've got to write to Dad, though," I said. "I'll do it as soon as we've finished."

I couldn't understand why Weezer was so quiet all the time we were drying the dishes and putting them away. I should have guessed that she was planning something, but I didn't. I only realized later on when she came into our room while I was writing my letter.

"Have you finished, Annie?" she asked, putting her head round the door. "Is it OK to talk to you?"

"Yes," I said,

"but just sit quietly for a second while I finish this picture off for Dad."

"What's it a picture of?" Weezer asked.

"It's Brad, fast asleep. Look."

Weezer looked. "I wish I could draw lovely pictures like you," she said. "Will you let me add a little note to Dad at the bottom of your letter?"

"OK," I said. "In a minute. Just wait till I've coloured Brad in."

"Right," said Weezer, stretching out on her bed. "I didn't just come in to chat. I want to discuss something with you." As she spoke, she kept raising and lowering one leg after the other into the air, toes pointed. "It's about this money thing."

"I thought we'd finished talking about that. There's not enough money for the seats you want and that's all there is to it. I'd go for the

gallery if I were you."

"You're not me," Weezer said. "Only a ballet dancer would understand why it's so important for me to see these Russian dancers close up. Anyway, it doesn't matter about Mum not being able to afford it, because I'm going to get enough all by myself. Well, with a bit of help from you, and Tony and Tricia and Maisie."

Brad's fur was all coloured in, so I put the lid on my brown felt-tip and took out a greeny-yellowy one for his eyes. "What are you talking about?" I said.

"I'm going to earn the money."

"How?"

"I'm going to hold a Jumble Sale."

"A Jumble Sale?"

"Yes, and then I think I'll put on a dancing show. Maybe Tony can be in some of the pieces as well."

"There's no room for dancing in our lounge," I said. "You'll look pretty silly all squashed in with the furniture."

"We could move the furniture," said Weezer, looking cross.

"It still wouldn't be right. And anyway, a lot of people aren't even that keen on ballet."

"I don't care about them," she said. "They're just stupid."

"You'll care if you don't get any money because nobody comes."

Weezer thought about this for a minute and sighed. "OK, I suppose you're right. What about a puppet show? I could do it with Tricia and Maisie. We've got loads of glove puppets. You could be in it too, if you like. We'll ask for 50p per ticket."

"Thanks," I said. "I think I'll just help with scenery and things."

"OK," said Weezer. "Whatever you like. And then I shall do all sorts of odd jobs for people too."

"I don't want to wash cars," I said.

"Well, there are lots of other things we could do."

"Like what?"

"Like walking people's dogs."

"There's not much time, though," I said. "The St Petersburg Ballet are coming the week after next, and don't forget that you go to ballet class on Tuesday afternoon and Saturday morning."

Weezer snorted. "As if I'd forget about ballet class! It's OK. We don't have to go to school next week. I've made up a timetable, look."

Weezer's timetable said:

'Saturday: start planning everything
Monday–Friday: do dog-walking
Wednesday: have Jumble Sale
Friday: have Puppet Show
Saturday: **GO AND BUY TICKETS!!!**'

I said, "If you're going to put on a puppet show in a week, you'd really better get cracking writing it."

"You're a good writer, Annie." Weezer was being specially nice. "Will you help me? We could do it now, before bedtime. It doesn't have to be a *long* puppet show."

"But it has to be good if you're going to charge people money to see it."

"It'll be ace if you write it, Annie. It'll be really brilliant."

If there's one thing my sister is good at, it's getting people to do what she wants. I put my felt-tips away and got my best notebook out.

"Come on," I said. "Let's make a list of everything we have to do."

I opened the notebook and wrote 'MONEY-MAKING' at the top of a new page.

Chapter Two

The next day was Saturday. When Weezer came back from her ballet class with Tony, she was frowning.

"I've been talking to Tony," she said. "I never realized that putting on a Puppet Show would be so fiddly. I never thought about how we're going to get everyone to come to it."

"I told you," said Tony. He almost lives at our house. He comes over every day to practise ballet with Weezer, and now he's like a sort of brother to us. He often has very good ideas. For instance, he seemed to know all about how to get people to watch our Puppet Show, and also how to get them to come to a Jumble Sale.

He said, "I'll print out something on our printer at home, and ask my dad if he'll make lots of copies for us."

"Won't he mind?" I asked.

"No, I'm sure he'll do it," Tony said.

"They've got a really good photocopier where he works. We also need tickets, but we can cut those out of ordinary paper and just write the price on them and sell them to everyone at the door."

"How many people do you think will come?" Weezer asked. "Do you think we can get twenty?"

"Twenty won't fit in your lounge," Tony said. "Maybe you should do two shows, one on Friday and one on Saturday."

"No," said Weezer. "We're going to get the tickets on Saturday. Everyone will just have to squash in, that's all. I'm going to tell the ballet class about it, so I'm sure lots of them will come."

"And I think," I said, "that we should put a note through all the letterboxes in this street asking everyone to give us their jumble."

"What about their dogs?" Weezer asked. "We'll have to knock on their doors for that, won't we?"

"I suppose so," I said. "But we'd better ask Mum about it first, to see if it's all right. I don't know how we're going to fit everything in. When are we going to rehearse the Puppet Show?"

"Have you written it?" Weezer asked.

"Not yet," I said. "You only told me about it yesterday."

"Well, if you can get it ready by Monday, then I'll invite Tricia and Maisie over for a rehearsal."

"OK," I said. "I'll go and start writing it, and you and Tony talk to Mum and then go and ask everyone about dogs and jumble. We can meet back here at suppertime and you can tell me all about it."

"No," said Weezer. "You've got to come and ask about the dogs. I can't go alone. People won't believe me on my own. They'll believe both of us. You can make it sound all grown-up and official."

"And I can't come," said Tony. "I'm going to put the advertisements on to the word-processor."

"So when am I supposed to write this play?" I asked.

"Later," said Weezer. "It won't take you long."

"All right," I said. "Let's go."

Weezer and I went from one house to another. We'd made a list with Mum of all the houses where she knew the people, and there

seemed to be lots of them. Some doors had brass knockers, others had electric bells which played a tune inside the house, and some people just had ordinary buzzer-type doorbells. I'd never realized how peculiar some of our neighbours were. Some people took ages and ages to understand what we were asking them for; others looked at us very

suspiciously, even though they must have known who we were. Lots of people thought we just wanted money to buy extra sweets with and didn't seem to believe Weezer when she explained to them about going to see *Coppélia*.

"Let's try Mrs Rosebush," she said. "They've got that pretty little dog." We didn't know what the Rosebushes' real name was, even though Mum often stopped to chat to them in the street. We called them that because they had rosebushes growing in big plant pots on either side of their front door. Weezer said this meant they were posh. I rang the doorbell, and the door opened straight away.

"Hello," I said.

"Hello, dear," said Mrs Rosebush. She was wearing a very fluffy pink jumper and her hair was very fluffy too, though it wasn't pink. "You're Mrs Blair's girls, aren't you?"

"Yes," said Weezer, "and we're trying to earn some extra money by taking dogs for walks."

"Could you do

it twice a day?" Mrs Rosebush asked. "Only I'm finding it a little difficult to get around . . .What about school?"

"It's half-term," Weezer said. I couldn't think why she'd asked me to come with her if she was going to do all the talking.

"We're charging a pound a day," I said. "That's for two walks, and we'd only be able to do it for next week, I'm afraid, because we're back at school the week after."

"That would be a great help to me," said Mrs Rosebush. "Could you come and collect Tilly at nine tomorrow?"

"Yes," I said. "Nine is fine. Thank you very much."

Weezer and I walked on to the next house. She was skipping along the pavement.

"Six pounds by Friday!" she sang. "We'll get the money in no time. We'll be rich! Maybe we'll even be able to afford a box."

By the end of the afternoon, we'd only found two more dogs who needed us, and the owners just wanted morning walks. Everyone else in our street seemed to have cats or rabbits or no pets at all. We went back to Tony's house to have a look at his advertisements.

"I've worked it out," Weezer told him, "that

the dog-walking will get us twelve pounds. That means we still need twenty-eight more. Will we be able to get that much from the Jumble Sale and Puppet Show?"

"You will after everyone sees my adverts," Tony said. "Look at this!" He put two sheets of paper on his desk. One said:

BRILLIANT PUPPET SHOW!!!
at
10 Ratcliffe Road
on
Friday February 15th
at
5.00 pm
EVERYONE WELCOME!
(Tickets at the door: 50p)

The other one said:

HAVE YOU GOT ANY JUMBLE?
We are holding a Jumble Sale
on
WEDNESDAY FEBRUARY 13TH
We will be collecting all unwanted
toys, books,
tapes, CDs, ornaments,
jewellery, scarves, etc.
on Sunday, 9th February.

The Jumble Sale will take place at
6.00 pm
on Wednesday, 13th February
at 10, Ratcliffe Road.

BRILLIANT BARGAINS FOR ALL!

"They look great!" said Weezer. "Everyone will want to come. And they'll give us tons of jumble, you'll see."

"Yes," I said. "They're lovely. But I don't think we should use 'brilliant' twice, do you, Tony?"

"What can we have instead?"

"How about 'Spectacular Puppet Show'?"

"Spectacular!" Weezer said. "Don't you think that's good, Tony?"

"OK," said Tony. "I can change it. It's easy." He sat down at the computer and started pressing buttons.

"And I'm not sure about calling it a Jumble Sale," I said.

"But is *is* a Jumble Sale!" Weezer said.

"Why don't we call it a Bring and Buy Sale?" I asked. "That sounds much more elegant."

"Does it?" She seemed uncertain. "Do you think it does, Tony?"

"Oh, yes," he said. "It definitely does."

"Right," said Weezer. "A Bring and Buy Sale, then. I'm going to phone Tricia and Maisie now and tell them all about the rehearsal on Monday."

"But I haven't written the play yet," I said.

"When are you going to do it, then?" Weezer asked. "There isn't much time."

"Now," I said. "I'm going home now, and I'll do it as quickly as I can."

"Tony and I will do some exercises while you write," said Weezer. "We haven't done enough barre work today."

They went off to dance and I started wondering what I was going to put into the Puppet Show.

Chapter Three

Weezer is in disgrace because of something she did at the Bring and Buy Sale. We had it in our house last night, at about six o'clock, and all the neighbours came because Tony had put one of his advertisements through lots and lots of letterboxes. We didn't make very much money because of Weezer. She was the one who said, "Everything's got to be dead cheap or no one will buy it."

In the end we only made £7.25 and that, added to the £12 from the dogwalking makes £19.25, so we still need lots more, and I'm sure we'll never get so many people coming to the Puppet Show. This is worrying me. Another thing that's worrying me is the Show itself. Every time I think of a story to write and show it to Weezer, she finds something wrong with it, and then I have to fiddle with it and fix it and show it to her again and it's all taking much longer than I thought it would. Tricia and

Maisie and Weezer all know what the characters in the story are. We've got five glove puppets:

1. A *dragon made from a green sock*
2. A *frog made of brown velvet*
3. A *knitted person called Stripy, because her body is knitted in red and blue stripes*
4. A *teddy bear called Mr Snuggly*
5. A *purple felt hippo called Horace*

It's very hard to think of a story they can all be in together, and I haven't had time to concentrate on it, because of being so busy, and because every time we have a spare moment, we seem to be walking the dogs. We only do it for twenty minutes each morning and for half an hour every afternoon. In the morning, we have three dogs (Tilly, Jess, and Pug) but only Tilly comes out with us in the afternoon. Yesterday Weezer said as we trudged around the pavements, "I never thought it would be as boring as this."

"What did you think would happen?" I said.

"I don't know . . . I thought perhaps the dogs would lead us into exciting adventures, or be naughty, or chase cats, or growl at little children. I just thought they'd do something interesting."

"Me too," I said, but the dogs were as well-behaved as could be, and trotted along quietly with Weezer and me hanging on tight to their leads, because, as Weezer put it, "We don't want them to run away. We'd never get our money if we lost the dogs."

We had also spent ages getting the Bring and Buy Sale ready.

"It's hard work, isn't it?" said Weezer. "Collecting all that stuff together. I thought it would be easy."

We had gone from house to house with a big black dustbin bag to hold all the jumble. Most people we spoke to hardly gave us anything.

"The NSPCC were collecting last week," someone said. "We gave them everything we had."

Other people said, "Well, I don't know if this will be of any use to you," and then they'd give us a lamp that didn't work, or some children's books with half the pages scribbled over in crayon, or jigsaw puzzles with some bits missing. Only Mrs Posnansky gave us anything pretty at all.

We had spread everything out on the carpet when we got home. Weezer said, "It all looks horrible. No one will want to buy this stuff. We're never going to get enough money. I think we should put in some of our own things as well."

"What things?" I said. "I don't want to sell my belongings."

"There must be something you don't want. Just have a look in your drawers. I'll go over and ask Tony too, and Mum might have some bits in the kitchen."

She went off to see them, and I was left alone to clean up the jumble we had managed to collect.

At about quarter to six last night, Weezer and I stood at the window of our front room and waited for the crowds to arrive. Brad was tiptoeing through the jumble, which was all neatly laid out on the dining-room table. He gave some ornaments a sniff, and was just starting to curl up for a nap on somebody's knitted tea-cosy when Weezer spotted him, and lifted him down to the floor.

"Sorry, Brad," she said. "You can't stay on the table. Someone might want to buy you to be their cat." Even Brad never argued with Weezer. He jumped up on to the windowsill and stared out at the street.

"Nobody's come yet," said Weezer. "Tony said he'd be here early."

"It's only just six, Weezer. Calm down," I said.

Mum was sitting on a chair at the front door, waiting to let people in. "I'll do door duty for half an hour and not a minute more," she'd told us. "At half past six I have to start cooking supper."

"Here they come!" Weezer shouted. "Maisie and Tricia and Mrs Posnansky and the couple from down the road with their little girl . . . it's going to be all right. Oh, Annie, it really is."

She was very nearly right.

The Bring and Buy Sale was almost a great success, except for what Weezer did. At first no one noticed. Everyone had left and Mum, Weezer and I were tidying up.

"We've got £12.25!" I told them. "Isn't that brilliant!"

"Well done, girls," said Mum. "I'm proud of you both." She turned to smile at Weezer, and then her smile turned into a frown.

"Where's my little china vase? The one that lives on the mantelpiece . . . I hope no one has bought it by mistake."

"I sold it!" Weezer said. "Wasn't that clever of me? I got five pounds for it from Mrs

Meadowes. Isn't that great?"

"You did WHAT?" Mum was so cross her face was quite white.

"Mrs Meadowes offered me five pounds for it, so I sold it to her. Five pounds, Mum. That's a fantastic amount of money. And you never

specially said you liked the vase."

"Well, I do," Mum said. "And you can just take this five-pound note and go round to Mrs Meadowes at once. Tell her you made a mistake and please could you have your mother's vase back. Go now. And I don't want to hear a single

solitary squeak out of you till that vase is back in this house. Annie, go with her please. It's too dark for her to go on her own."

On the way over to Mrs Meadowes' house, Weezer said, "We've only got £7.25 now. I don't see why Mum is making such a fuss about a silly old vase."

"She likes it," I told her. "You shouldn't have sold it, Weezer. You know you shouldn't. You wouldn't like it if someone sold your ballet shoes."

Weezer snorted. "Ballet shoes aren't at all the same thing. I *need* my ballet shoes."

"Maybe Mum needs her vase."

"What for? She never puts flowers in it, not ever. It just sits there."

"I don't know . . . Anyway, it's not that she needs it; nobody really *needs* a vase. But she likes it, so you shouldn't have sold it, and that's that. Now, this is Mrs Meadowes' house. You knock."

We got the vase back, but Mrs Meadowes made quite a fuss, and when we came back, Mum sent Weezer to our room in disgrace. I wasn't allowed in there till bedtime, so I sat at the kitchen table, putting the finishing touches to the Puppet Show, ready to show Weezer when I went upstairs.

Chapter Four

"This is all wrong!" Weezer said. "This Puppet Show is not going to work. We haven't had enough rehearsal."

"It's not our fault," said Tricia. "We came on Monday and the play wasn't ready yet."

"Then we came on Wednesday morning, and you were all busy with the Jumble Sale," said Maisie.

"Bring and Buy," Weezer sighed. "I know. We've only really been doing it since yesterday, but everyone's coming in two hours, and we're not nearly good enough yet."

"Don't worry, Weezer," Tony said. "It'll be fine. I'll be the director and tell you what you're doing wrong."

"I won't even let you watch," Weezer said, "if you call me 'Weezer'. You know what my name is."

"Oh, all right, then," said Tony, "Louisa, if you insist."

"Right," I said. "Let's start again."

Weezer, Tricia and Maisie went behind the sofa and put their glove puppets on. I'd written a story about a dragon who ate teddy bears for his tea, and a teddy bear who wanted to be a hero and kill the dragon. This teddy bear had two friends, a frog and a hippo, who were timid and kept playing tricks on him to stop him from climbing into the dragon's cave. Teddy wouldn't be stopped, and in the end he did kill the dragon and then he got married to Stripy, who was being a sort of knitted princess. It was a very silly story. I'd written all sorts of bits for people to say and even a song for Teddy to sing. It went like this:

"I'm going to kill the dragon,
the dragon I'm going to kill,
as soon as I've pulled my wagon,
to the top of Dragon Hill."

Weezer, who was being Teddy, refused to sing it.

"We haven't got a hill," she said. "We're all up on the back of the sofa together. I'm not singing a song about a hill that isn't even there. And we haven't got a wagon. It's stupid to sing a song about stuff that's invisible. What will the audience think?"

"People," I said, "will have to use their imaginations." But I could see what she meant.

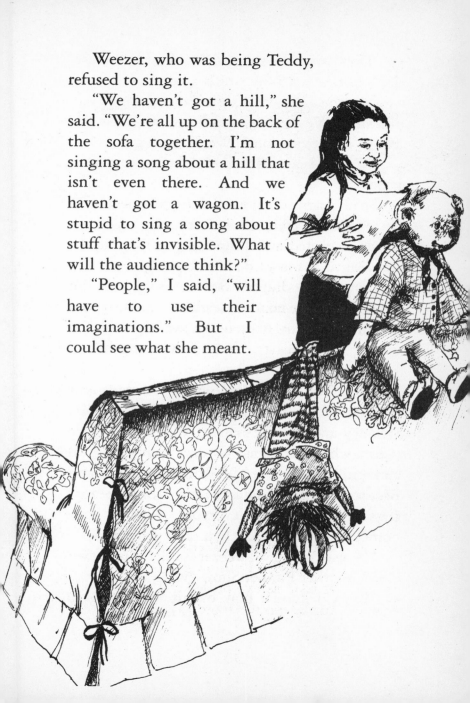

"Don't sing the song, then," I said. "In fact, don't bother with my words at all."

"You mean make it up as we go along? Are you sure? We do that at ballet sometimes. We call it 'improvisation'," Weezer said grandly.

"Try it," I said. "It couldn't be worse than it is now."

I had to admit that everything sounded much better when everyone was making up their own words. I cheered myself up by imagining myself standing at our front door and saying:

"Sorry! The Puppet Show is sold out, I'm afraid. There are no more seats left . . . Oh, you'd be willing to pay to stand at the back . . . Oh well, in that case, sir, thank you very much."

The Puppet Show was a disaster. We made four pounds. Not counting Mum and Mr and Mrs Delaney and Mrs Posnansky, only four people came who were, as Weezer put it, 'real audience'. They were Mrs Rosebush, Linda and Pam from ballet class, and Daisy from Weezer's class at school. After everyone else had gone home, we sat at the kitchen table with Tony.

"It was awful," Weezer said. "I'm never doing another Puppet Show ever."

"If we'd known how bad it was going to

be," said Tony, "we could have sold the puppets at the Bring and Buy and made a bit more money."

"Not much use having good ideas now, though, is it?" said Weezer. "The Bring and Buy Sale is over and so is the Puppet Show and we still haven't got the money we need . . . even with the boring dog-walking."

Weezer's face was looking more and more frowny, and her mouth was starting to turn down at the corners. I said, "Cheer up, Louisa." (I was careful about her name.) "Let's make a list of all the money we've got."

"We know how much money we've got," she said.

"But it looks better if you write it down," I said. I took a clean piece of paper and made a list.

- DOGWALKING   £12.00
- BRING AND BUY   £7.25
- PUPPET SHOW   £4.00

- TOTAL   £23.25

- NEEDED FOR TICKETS £40.00
- STILL TO GET   £16.75

We all stared at the figures.

"We can't go and that's that," Weezer said. "We still need more than fifteen pounds. Don't forget we need money for the bus fares as well."

"And we have to have the money by tomorrow," I said, "because that's when we're going to buy the tickets."

Weezer was looking more and more as if she was about to burst into tears. As I was wondering what to say, Mum came into the kitchen. She was carrying her purse.

"I've just been on the phone to your dad," she said. "I told him you were busy so he's ringing back later to chat to you both, but he did tell me to give you any money that you needed to make up the ticket prices. £20, is it? Or £15?"

"It's exactly £17.55, including bus fares," I said, and Mum opened the purse and put the money down in front of Weezer.

"There we are," she said. "Two front stall seats for Louisa Ballerina and her sister . . . You *shall* go to the ball, Cinders!"

Weezer jumped up and hugged Mum.

"That's brilliant, Mum," she said. "Thank you, thank you, thank you all there is! I'm so happy!" She beamed at us. "You get extra happy, don't you, when you've just been feeling miserable and then it stops?"

Tony and I both agreed that you did. I was pleased about the money, of course, and about going to the ballet, but best of all was not having to do all sorts of things like collecting jumble and writing plays for puppets which then never got used, and walking dogs. The last week had been so busy that I was quite looking forward to going back to school, where I could have a bit of a rest.

Chapter Five

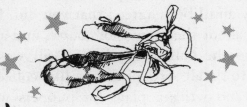

Weezer spent the whole of the bus ride from our house to the theatre telling me the story of *Coppélia*. She came tearing back from her ballet class at lunchtime and could hardly eat anything at all because she was so excited.

"Have you got the money, Annie?" she kept asking me, and I kept having to get my purse out of my jacket pocket and showing her the four ten-pound notes that Mum had given me in exchange for all our odd pound coins and bits of change.

"Take care of it," Mum had said to me. "Keep your pocket zipped up and be careful of the traffic. Hold Weezer's hand crossing the road. You know she's quite capable of doing arabesques in the middle of all the cars if the mood is on her."

"I'm not stupid," Weezer had said. "I'd never do anything like that."

I said to Weezer, "Stop worrying. I won't

lose the money," and she said, "OK, I will stop worrying. I'll tell you the story of *Coppélia* instead."

So there we were on the bus and Weezer was talking, and I wasn't really listening to her properly. I was staring out of the window and pieces of the story floated into my ears from time to time.

"A spooky doctor who makes a doll . . . his name is Coppélius, so the doll's called Coppélia . . . she's so real that the hero, Fritz, falls in love with her . . . but Fritz's girlfriend, Swanilda, plays a trick on him . . . she dresses up in the doll's clothes and the Doctor thinks it's real magic and she's come alive . . . it all ends happily, though. When you see it, it'll all be much clearer. The music's lovely. Are we nearly there?"

"Yes," I said, "Come on, we're getting off now."

"Yippee!" Weezer said and everyone on the bus turned to look at us.

"I don't care," she whispered to me. "I'm going to get tickets for the ballet."

The Theatre Royal had thick red carpets in the foyer.

"There," said Weezer. "That's the Box Office."

"It looks more like a cage than a box," I said. "Look at the gold bars. The ladies who work there must feel as though they're in a zoo or something."

Weezer giggled. "We could feed them bananas through the bars."

"Ssh!" I said. "Behave yourself. I'm going to

queue up now."

We had to wait about ten minutes until it was our turn.

"Yes, dear," said the lady behind the bars. "What can I do for you?"

"I'd like two tickets for *Coppélia* for next Saturday's matinée, please," I said.

"It's sold out, I'm afraid," said the lady.

"Sold out? What does that mean?"

"We have no more tickets for the Russian Ballet left at all. Every single performance has been sold out since last week. I'm very sorry."

"Even the seats in the gallery?"

"Even those, I'm afraid. There's just nothing more available. I'm really very sorry."

Suddenly I felt cold and sick and I didn't dare to look at Weezer, but of course I had to. What would I do if she burst into tears? If she did, I knew she wouldn't stop for ages. I took a deep breath.

"Weezer," I said and then nearly bit my tongue. What a time to get my sister's name wrong! But Weezer was so unhappy that she didn't even notice.

"Don't say a word, Annie," she said to me. "I don't want to talk about it. Not ever."

She stalked out of the theatre and I ran after

her. "Wait!" I shouted. "Don't cross the road without me!"

She gave me her hand in silence and all the way home she didn't make a single sound, but sat staring down at the space between her feet, her face as stiff and white as a doll's.

She went on being silent as we walked home from the bus stop. Usually, when Weezer's miserable, I can cheer her up by chatting to her, or else I can make her laugh by telling her a joke, but I knew that she was so upset now that any words I might say to her would be the wrong ones.

Mrs Posnansky was coming out of our gate as we got to our house.

"It is my Little Swan and her sister!" she said. "I am come to invite you to my house. There is a guest there I wish for you both to meet."

Mrs Posnansky's words were like a spell. Before she'd finished speaking, Weezer had opened her mouth and begun to howl. It was just as if she'd been keeping all her sadness locked up somewhere, and Mrs Posnansky had turned a magical key. Tears poured down Weezer's cheeks. I think the noises coming out of her mouth were what's called 'wailing' in stories. I'd never heard her make these sounds before.

I didn't know what to do, but Mrs Posnansky did. She said to me, "Annie, darling, go and tell your mama you are having tea in my house. I will deal with this."

She put her arms round Weezer and led her away, still wailing and sobbing.

Mum opened our door as soon as I knocked and said, "What's happened, Annie?"

I told her everything, and I couldn't believe how calm she was about it. I expected her to want to rush off to Mrs Posnansky's and cuddle

Weezer to make her feel better, but all she did was smile mysteriously and say, "Well, that's very interesting, Annie, but Mrs Posnansky was here to invite you both to tea, so you'd better go over and keep Weezer company."

"Weezer isn't much company when she's in a state. I'll have to do all the talking on my own."

"Oh, I don't know about that," said Mum, even more mysteriously. "Go on. They'll be waiting for you."

Mrs Posnansky's house is full of lovely things to look at. She has more ornaments on her shelves than anyone I know, and lots of framed photographs hanging on her walls. Her mother was a ballet dancer, long ago, and this means that she and Weezer always have a lot to chat about. Weezer shows Mrs Posnansky every new step she learns in class, and the feathered headdress Mrs Posnansky gave her when she was a Little Swan is Weezer's most treasured possession.

"Come in, come in, Annie," Mrs Posnansky said as she opened the door. "There is someone here I wish you to meet. He is good friend of mine from the old country, from Russia. Oh, we have many, many things to talk about!"

"Where's Weezer?" I asked. "Is she all right? Is she still crying?"

"No, no," said Mrs Posnansky. "She talks with my friend. The feathers of the Little Swan are no longer in a ruffle. They are smooth and white. She is quite calm."

"How did you manage it?" I whispered. "She was so upset."

"I did nothing. It is my friend."

We walked into the lounge. There was a man with white hair sitting on the sofa. Weezer was sitting next to him, chatting away happily.

"Hello," I said. Weezer jumped up and grabbed my hand and pulled me over to the sofa.

"Annie," she said. "Oh, Annie, you'll never guess! This is Alexander Petrov. It really, really is him! It's fantastic."

I was obviously meant to know who this person was, but I'd never heard of him.

"Hello," I said, feeling rather shy. He looked just like a king. He was quite old, but his eyes were very blue and twinkly and he wore a beautiful velvet waistcoat and sat up very straight.

Mrs Posnansky saw that I didn't know who he was, because she said, "This is Sasha. I call him this from when we were small. It is Russian short name for Alexander. Everyone else has to call him 'Maestro' because he is now Big Boss."

"Oh," I said. I still didn't know who he was.

Weezer helped me. She said, "Annie, Mr Petrov is the Director of the St Petersburg Ballet Company . . . the ones who are doing *Coppélia*."

"And you are Louisa's sister, Annie," he said to me. "I am enchanted. Your sister has told me you are trying to come to *Coppélia*."

"Oh, yes," I said. "But all the tickets have gone."

I looked at Weezer to see how she would react, but she looked perfectly calm so I went on, "We're very sad about it."

"No more need for sadness," said Mr Petrov, and waved his hand in the air in a very grand way. "You come to the matinée next Saturday as my guests. You and Louisa . . . I will make very big surprise."

"Isn't it brilliant, Annie?" Weezer squeaked. "I can't wait. I'm so excited I don't think I'll be able to sleep."

She took my hands and actually began to jump for joy. I'd never seen anyone really do that before, but Weezer was doing it. It was only when Mrs Posnansky brought in a Black Forest gâteau that she quietened down and sat on the sofa again.

Chapter Six

"I expect," Weezer said, "that this is what princesses must feel like. Don't you think, Annie?"

I nodded. Weezer had certainly done her best to dress like a princess. She'd insisted on wearing her very best party dress, even though it was only lunchtime, and she'd made me put on my best clothes as well. My dress wasn't as frilly and princessy as hers was, but I still felt ridiculous wearing blue velvet just to go to the theatre. I'd said so to Weezer as we got ready. She was changing out of her leotard. The Saturday ballet class had been cancelled, and so my sister had made up for it by dancing in the lounge. She'd put on her *Coppélia* tape, and I guessed that she was pretending to be Swanilda. She wouldn't let anyone watch her, which wasn't a bit like Weezer. By the time she came up to change, I was nearly ready. I said,

"I feel a bit stupid wearing this dress."

"We have to wear our best things," Weezer said firmly. "We're the Maestro's guests. And it's a ballet, not a movie or something. And he's sending a special car for us."

"It's not really for us," I said. "It's for Mrs Posnansky. If it was just us going, I'm sure he'd have let us go on the bus."

"Still, we get to go with her, don't we?" said Weezer. "We can pretend it's our car."

"Did you hear him calling her Ninotchka?" I asked Weezer. "I bet he's in love with her."

"You think everyone's in love with everyone else. It's just stupid. He hasn't got time to be in love. He's the director of a Ballet Company."

I had to admit that it was very grand riding through town in a big, shiny black car.

"Why do you think we have to be there so early?" Weezer asked me. "It's one o'clock now and the show doesn't start till half past two. Do *you* know, Mrs Posnansky?"

"I know nothing," said Mrs Posnansky, who was wearing the same sparkly sequinned scarf that she'd worn to Weezer's Dancing Display. "Only that Sasha says we must go to stage door."

If you weren't looking for it, it would have

been easy to miss the stage door completely. It was just a dull brown wooden door down an alley that ran along the side of the theatre.

"Come," said Mrs Posnansky and opened it, looking as though she knew exactly where to go and what to do.

"Imagine," said Weezer, "if we'd been by ourselves. We'd never have dared to go in like that."

A fat, bald man was sitting just inside the door.

"We are guests of Mr Petrov," said Mrs Posnansky. "He expects, I think."

The fat man looked at a list on a clipboard. "Mrs Posnansky, Miss Louisa Blair and Miss Anna Blair."

"Anne," I said, "or Annie," but no one heard me, and I didn't really mind. I quite like Anna.

"We're on a list!" Weezer whispered. "In a real theatre. I feel like one of the dancers."

"This corridor isn't what I imagined a theatre would look like," I said.

"Why? What did you expect?"

"I don't know. Something smarter, more glamorous. A bit more like the front. I thought there would be carpets."

While Weezer and I were talking, the fat

man was speaking into a sort of telephone. He looked up at Mrs Posnansky and said, "Maestro is waiting in Dressing Room 3. That's along the corridor, down some steps, and then turn right. You can't miss it."

The corridor was very narrow. We had to press ourselves against the wall to let some people pass us. They were all wearing jeans and sweaters and trainers, but Weezer said, "Those are dancers. I can tell, just by the way they walk."

"How can you tell?" I said.

She never had time to answer, because Mrs Posnansky was knocking on the door of Dressing Room 3. The Maestro himself opened it and beamed at all of us.

"Ah, it is you, Ninotchka, my dear, and the two young ladies. Come in, come in. This is the dressing room of Sergei, who is dancing Doctor Coppélius. See, he is already partly in costume and looks like half an old man!"

Weezer's mouth was open, and her eyes were wide. Sergei stood up and bowed to us, and we could see that he was in the middle of doing his make-up and had drawn frown lines on his forehead and big black rings under his eyes.

"I am the Doctor," he said. "At your service.

See!" He picked up a wig of white hair with a plastic bald patch in the middle, and pulled it on over his own hair, which was reddish-brown. "A magical transformation."

Weezer still hadn't said anything. She was gazing at the costumes, hanging on a rail; at the mirror with light bulbs all around it; at the sticks of make-up lying on the table; at the many pairs of ballet shoes piled up beside the armchair.

"We let him dress now," said the Maestro. "There is much for us to see. Sergei will meet us on the stage."

"Are we going on the stage?" Weezer asked. "Is it allowed?"

The Maestro laughed. "If I allow it, it is allowed. But first, we meet the ladies."

We went into a huge dressing room in which about ten dancers were putting on make-up, sitting at a dressing table that took up a whole wall. Their pale mauve tutus were hanging up, ready for them to put on.

"This young lady," said the Maestro, pointing at Weezer, "wishes to be ballerina."

All the dancers smiled at us, and one of them pulled Weezer to her side. She put some blusher on her cheeks, and a little lipstick on her mouth.

"Thank you!" Weezer was breathless. "How lovely! I can't wait to see you in the show. Your tutus are so beautiful!"

"Take!" said the dancer who'd put on Weezer's make-up. "Take a flower, please!"

She took three yellow roses from a vase on the dressing-table and gave one each to Weezer and me and Mrs Posnansky. Weezer flung her arms around the dancer's neck and hugged her.

"Thank you! I wish I could be exactly like you when I grow up. Please tell me what your name is."

"Is Galina. You have heard

of famous prima ballerina, Galina Ulanova?"

"Oh yes," said Weezer. "Of course I have."

"My parents, they call me Galina after her."

"My name," said Weezer, "is Louisa."

"That is very good name for ballerina," said Galina. "Very romantic."

Weezer was practically walking on air when we left. "See?" she said. "See what Galina said? I *knew* Louisa was a good name."

"Come," said Mrs Posnansky. "I take the roses to look after them till we are at home."

We made our way behind the back-cloth, stepping carefully over cables and ropes and making sure not to bump into the backs of bits of scenery.

"This," said the Maestro, showing us a big cupboard made of painted cardboard, "is the place where the Doctor hides his doll, his Coppélia.

And this," he led us on to the stage, "is the Village Square. There," he pointed, "is the balcony of the Doctor's house."

"And here I am," said Sergei, and hobbled out on to the dimly-lit stage.

"Oh!" said Weezer. "You look so old."

"Come," said Sergei. "We will dance together."

"Me?" Weezer looked at me, then at Mrs Posnansky, then at the Maestro.

"Of course you," said Sergei. "The Maestro has told me you are dancer."

Weezer said, "I'm learning. But I know Swanilda's dance from *Coppélia*."

"Really? This you have learned already? Is very advanced."

"No," said Weezer. "I haven't learned it in class, but I've watched the video so many times. I can't do it properly, of course. I'm not allowed up on points yet."

"Let me see, please," said Sergei.

Weezer began to dance. She was never shy about dancing. You only had to ask her once and she'd begin. She didn't even need music. It was true that she *did* spend ages and ages watching her ballet videos, but I never realized that she was learning the steps as she watched.

Now she was a doll, bending her head to one side, moving her arms and legs stiffly but gracefully, bowing from the waist, turning like a clockwork toy. I remembered all over again how I felt when I saw Weezer being a Little Swan: amazed that my sister (who could be so annoying sometimes) could turn herself into all these different and wonderful shapes. It was like watching a sort of magic.

"Bravo!" said Sergei and the Maestro, and Mrs Posnansky's eyes were all glittery. Ballet always made her cry, she said, because it was so beautiful.

"We do *pas de deux* now," said Sergei, and he took Weezer's hand and they did a little dance together, with Weezer still pretending to be a doll and Sergei being Doctor Coppélius.

"Enough!" said the Maestro after a few minutes. "You, Sergei, must rest till your entrance, and ladies, you must come with me. I have to show you to your seats. Oh, very special seats I have for you today. And come, please, to my office in the interval. I have ordered ice cream, naturally.

"Goodbye, ladies, goodbye, little ballerina," said Sergei. "It was for me a great pleasure to meet you."

We all said goodbye, and Weezer stared after him as he left. Mrs Posnansky and I followed the Maestro off the stage, and it wasn't till we were in the wings that I noticed that Weezer wasn't with us. She was still standing in the middle of the stage.

"Hey!" I whispered. "Come on! You're not supposed to be on stage now."

"I'm coming," she said. "I'm coming now."

She blew a kiss to an imaginary audience and then made a very low curtsey. I knew she was hearing applause in her head. She clutched an invisible bunch of flowers to her as she ran off stage.

"Wasn't it marvellous?" she whispered to me. "I'll never forget it. Never. And listen, the orchestra is tuning up. Oh, Annie, it's just like a dream, isn't it?"

"Please to sit, Louisa," said the Maestro. "And Annie, and you, my dear Ninotchka. It is not the most comfortable chair, but you see everything."

We took our places on three small stools in the wings, hidden behind the red velvet curtains.

"We're in the wings, Annie," Weezer said just before the curtain went up. "Actually on

the stage. It's almost as if we're part of the company. Ssh! It's going to start."

The stage was suddenly bright, and a line of dancers came running into the yellow light. I noticed Galina, and turned to see if Weezer had spotted her, but my sister was sitting so still and watching so carefully that I didn't dare to break the spell.

At the end of the first act, we made our way to the Maestro's office.

"I was in the wings, Annie," Weezer said to me, "but soon I'm going to be out there on the stage. Wait and see."

"I know you will," I said, and I *did* know it. That was where Weezer belonged: in the spotlight. "Let's go and get that ice cream."

ABOUT THE AUTHOR

Adèle Geras has written more than eighty books for children and young adults. These include *Troy* (Highly Commended for the Carnegie Medal) and the *Egerton Hall Trilogy*. She lives in Manchester with her husband and they have two daughters and a granddaughter.

www.adelegeras.com